Dear Reader,

Looking back over the years, I find it hard to realise that twenty-six of them have gone by since I wrote my first book—*Sister Peters in Amsterdam*. It wasn't until I started writing about her that I found that once I had started writing, nothing was going to make me stop—and at that time I had no intention of sending it to a publisher. It was my daughter who urged me to try my luck.

I shall never forget the thrill of having my first book accepted. A thrill I still get each time a new story is accepted. Writing to me is such a pleasure, and seeing a story unfolding on my old typewriter is like watching a film and wondering how it will end. Happily of course.

To have so many of my books re-published is such a delightful thing to happen and I can only hope that those who read them will share my pleasure in seeing them on the bookshelves again. . .and enjoy reading them.

Back by Popular Demand

A collector's edition of favourite titles from one of the world's best-loved romance authors. Mills & Boon are proud to bring back these sought after titles and present them as one cherished collection.

BETTY NEELS: COLLECTOR'S EDITION

ROSES FOR CHRISTMAS

BY
BETTY NEELS

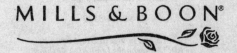

MILLS & BOON®

MILLS & BOON and MILLS & BOON with the Rose Device are registered trademarks of the publisher.

First published in Great Britain 1975 by Mills & Boon Limited
This edition 1996
Harlequin Mills & Boon Limited,
Eton House, 18-24 Paradise Road, Richmond, Surrey, TW9 1SR

© Betty Neels 1975

ISBN 0 263 79896 8

Set in Times Roman 12 on 13 pt by
Rowland Phototypesetting Limited
Bury St Edmunds, Suffolk

73-9612-43329

Printed and bound in Great Britain
by BPC Paperbacks Limited, Aylesbury

CHAPTER ONE

THE loft was warm, dusty and redolent of apples; the autumn sunshine peeping through its one dusty window tinted the odds and ends hanging on the walls with golden light, so that the strings of onions, cast-off skates, old raincoats, lengths of rope, worn-out leather straps and an old hat or two had acquired a gilded patina. Most of the bare floor was taken up with orderly rows of apples, arranged according to their kind, but there was still space enough left for the girl sitting in the centre, a half-eaten apple in one hand, the other buried in the old hat box beside her. She was a pretty girl, with light brown hair and large hazel eyes, extravagantly lashed and heavily browed, and with a straight nose above a generous, nicely curved mouth. She was wearing slacks and a thick, shabby sweater, and her hair, tied back none too tidily, hung down her back almost to her waist.

She bit into her apple and then bent over the box, and its occupant, a cat of plebeian appearance, paused in her round-the-clock washing of four kittens to lick the hand instead. The girl smiled and took another bite of apple, then turned to look behind her, to where a ladder led down to the disused stable below. She knew the footsteps climbing it and sighed to herself; holidays were lovely after the bustle and orderly precision of the ward in the big Edinburgh hospital where she was a Sister; the cosy homeliness of the manse where her parents and five brothers and sisters lived in the tiny village on the northernmost coast of Scotland, was bliss, it was only a pity that on this particular week's holiday, both her elder brothers, James and Donald, should be away from home, leaving Henry, the youngest and only eight years old, recovering from chickenpox, with no one to amuse him but herself. She doted on him, but they had been fishing all the morning, and after lunch had been cleared away she had gone to the loft for an hour's peace before getting the tea, and now here he was again, no doubt with some boyish scheme or other which would probably entail climbing trees or walking miles looking for seashells.

His untidy head appeared at the top of the ladder. 'I knew you'd be here, Eleanor,' he said in a satisfied voice. 'There's something I must tell you—it's most exciting.'

'Margaret's home early from school?'

He gave her a scornful look, still standing some way down the ladder so that only his head was visible. 'That's not exciting—she comes home from school every day—besides, she's only my sister.'

Eleanor trimmed the core of her apple with her nice white teeth. 'I'm your sister, Henry.'

'But you're old. . .'

She nodded cheerfully. 'Indeed I am, getting on for twenty-five, my dear. Tell me the exciting news.'

'Someone's come—Mother's invited him to tea.'

Eleanor's eyebrows rose protestingly. 'Old Mr MacKenzie? Not again?'

Her small brother drew a deep breath. 'You'll never guess.'

She reached over for another apple. 'Not in a thousand years—you'd better tell me before I die of curiosity.'

'It's Fulk van Hensum.'

'Fulk? Him? What's he here for? It's twenty years. . .' She turned her back on her brother, took a bite of apple and said with her mouth full: 'Tell Mother that I can't possibly come—I don't want to waste time talking to him; he was a horrid boy and I daresay he's grown into a horrid man. He pulled my hair. . .nasty arrogant type, I've never forgotten him.'

'I've never forgotten you, either, Eleanor.' The voice made her spin round. In place of Henry's head was the top half of a very large man; the rest of him came into view as she stared, so tall and broad that he was forced to bend his elegantly clad person to avoid bumping his head. He was very dark, with almost black hair and brown eyes under splendid eyebrows; his nose was long and beaky with winged nostrils, and his mouth was very firm.

Eleanor swallowed her apple. 'Well, I never!' she declared. 'Haven't you grown?'

He sat down on a convenient sack of potatoes and surveyed her lazily. 'One does, you know, and you, if I might say so, have become quite a big girl, Eleanor.'

He somehow managed to convey the impression that she was outsized, and she flushed a little; her father always described her as a fine figure of a woman, an old-fashioned phrase which she had accepted as a compliment, but to be called quite a big girl in that nasty drawling voice was decidedly annoying. She frowned at him and he remarked lightly: 'Otherwise you haven't changed, dear girl—still the heavy frown, I see—and the biting comment. Should I be flattered that you still remember me?'

'No.'

'Could we let bygones be bygones after—let me see, twenty years?'

She didn't answer that, but: 'You've been a great success, haven't you? We hear about you, you know; Father holds you up as a shining example to Donald.'

'Donald? Ah, the medical student. I'm flattered. What's in the box?'

'Mrs Trot and her four kittens.'

He got up and came to sit beside her with the box between them, and when he offered a large, gentle hand, the little cat licked it too.

'Nice little beast. Don't you want to know why I'm here?' He chose an apple with care and began to eat it. 'How peaceful it is,' he observed. 'What are you doing now, Eleanor? Still a nurse?'

She nodded. 'In Edinburgh, but I'm on a week's holiday.'

'Not married yet?' And when she shook her head: 'Engaged?'

'No—are you?'

'Married? No. Engaged, yes.'

For some reason she felt upset, which was ridiculous, because for all these years she had remembered him as someone she didn't like—true, she had been barely five years old at their first meeting and tastes as well as people change; all the same, there was no need for her to feel so put out at his news.

She asked the inevitable female question: 'Is she pretty?'

The dark eyes looked at her thoughtfully. 'Yes, ethereal—very small, slim, fair hair, blue eyes—she dresses with exquisite taste.'

Eleanor didn't look at him. She tucked Mrs Trot up in her old blanket and got to her feet, feeling, for some reason, a much bigger girl than she actually was and most regrettably shabby and untidy. Not that it mattered, she told herself crossly; if people came calling without warning they could take her as they found her. She said haughtily: 'Tea will be ready, I expect,' and went down the ladder with the expertise of long practice. She waited politely for him at the bottom and then walked beside him out of the stable and across the cobbled yard towards the house. She walked well, her head well up and with a complete lack of self-consciousness, for she was a graceful girl despite her splendid proportions and tall, although now her head barely reached her companion's shoulder.

'It hasn't changed,' her companion observed, looking around him. 'I'm glad my father came just once again before he died; he loved this place. It was a kind of annual pilgrimage with him, wasn't it?'

Eleanor glanced up briefly. 'Yes—we were all sorry when he died, we all knew him

so well, and coming every year as he did. . .'
She paused and then went on: 'You never
came, and now after all these years you
have. Why?'

They had stopped in the open back porch
and he answered her casually: 'Oh, one
reason and another, you know.' He was eye-
ing her in a leisurely fashion which she found
annoying. 'Do you always dress like this?'

She tossed back her mane of hair. 'You
haven't changed at all,' she told him tartly.
'You're just as hateful as you were as a boy.'

He smiled. 'You have a long memory.'
His dark eyes snapped with amusement. 'But
then so have I, Eleanor.'

She led the way down the flagstoned passage and opened a door, while vivid memory
came flooding back—all those years ago,
when he had picked her up and held her
gently while she howled and sobbed into his
shoulder and even while she had hated him
then, just for those few minutes she had felt
secure and content and very happy despite
the fact that moments earlier she had been
kicking his shins—she had lost her balance
and fallen over and he had laughed, but
gently, and picked her up. . .it was silly to
remember such a trivial episode from her
childhood.

The sitting room they entered wasn't large,

but its heterogeneous mixture of unassuming antiques and comfortable, shabby armchairs, handmade rugs and bookshelves rendered it pleasant enough. It had two occupants: Eleanor's mother, a small, pretty woman, very neatly dressed, and her father, a good deal older than his wife, with thick white hair and bright blue eyes in a rugged face. He was in elderly grey tweeds and only his dog collar proclaimed his profession.

'There you are,' exclaimed Mrs MacFarlane. 'So you found each other.' She beamed at them both. 'Isn't it nice to meet again after all these years? Fulk, come and sit here by me and tell me all your news,' and when he had done so: 'Did you recognise Eleanor? She was such a little girl when you last saw her.'

Eleanor was handing plates and teacups and saucers. 'Of course he didn't recognise me, Mother,' she explained in a brisk no-nonsense voice. 'I was only five then, and that's twenty years ago.'

'A nice plump little thing you were, too,' said her father fondly, and smiled at their guest, who remarked blandly: 'Little girls so often are,' and Eleanor, although she wasn't looking at him, knew that he was secretly laughing. It was perhaps fortunate that at that moment Henry joined them, to sit himself down as close to him as possible.

'Are you going to stay here?' he enquired eagerly. 'I mean, for a day or two? And must I call you Doctor van Hensum, and will you. . .?'

'Call me Fulk, Henry, and yes, your mother has very kindly asked me to stay for a short visit.'

'Oh, good—you can come fishing with us, Eleanor and me, you know, and there's an apple tree she climbs, I daresay she'll let you climb it too if you like.'

'Eat your bread and butter, Henry,' said Eleanor in the same brisk voice. 'I'm sure Doctor van Hensum doesn't climb trees at his age, and probably he's not in the least interested in fishing.' She cast the doctor a smouldering glance. 'He may want to rest. . .'

She caught the quick gleam in his eyes although his voice was meek enough. 'As to that, I'm only thirty-six, you know, and reasonably active.'

'Of course you are,' declared Mrs MacFarlane comfortably, and passed him the cake. 'I can remember you fishing, too—and climbing trees—Eleanor used to shriek at you because you wouldn't let her climb trees too.' She laughed at the memory and her daughter ground her splendid teeth. 'So long ago,' sighed her mother, 'and I remember it all so vividly.'

And that was the trouble, Eleanor told herself, although why the memory was so vivid was a mystery beyond her.

'And now,' interpolated her father, 'you are a famous physician; of course your dear father was a brilliant man—you were bound to follow in his footsteps, and your mother was a clever woman too, and an uncommonly pretty one. I'm afraid that we none of us can hold a candle to your splendid career, although Eleanor has done very well for herself, you know; in her own small sphere she has specialized in medicine and is very highly thought of at her hospital, so I'm told.' He added with a touch of pride: 'She's a Ward Sister—one of the youngest there.'

'I can hardly believe it,' observed Fulk, and only she realized that he was referring to her careless appearance; no one, seeing her at that moment would have believed that she was one and the same person as the immaculately uniformed, highly professional young woman who ruled her ward so precisely. A pity he can't see me on duty, she thought peevishly, and said aloud: 'Donald—he's younger than I—is at Aberdeen and doing very well. He's going in for surgery.'

She encountered the doctor's gaze again and fidgeted under it. 'He was in his pram when you were here.'

He said smoothly: 'Ah, yes, I remember. Father always kept me up to date with any news about you; there's Mary—she's married, isn't she? and Margaret?'

'Here she is now,' said Mrs MacFarlane, 'back from school—and don't forget James, he's still at boarding school.' She cast a fond look at her last-born, gobbling cake. 'Henry's only home because he's had chickenpox.'

There was a small stir as Margaret came in. She was already pretty and at twelve years old bade fair to outshine Eleanor later on. She embraced her mother, declaring she was famished, assured Eleanor that she would need help with her homework and went to kiss her father. She saw the doctor then and said instantly: 'Is that your car in the lane? It's absolutely wizard!'

Her father's voice was mildly rebuking. 'This is Fulk van Hensum, Margaret, he used to come and stay with us a long time ago— you remember his father? He is to stay with us for a day or so.'

She shook hands, smiling widely. 'Oh, yes—I remember your father and I know about you too.' She eyed him with some curiosity. 'You're very large, aren't you?'

He smiled slowly. 'I suppose I am. Yes, that's my car outside—it's a Panther de Ville.'

It was Henry who answered him. 'I say, is it really? May I look at it after tea? There are only a few built, aren't there—it's rather like an XJ12, isn't it? With a Jag engine. . .'

The big man gave him a kindly look. 'A motorcar enthusiast?' he wanted to know, and when Henry nodded, 'We'll go over it presently if you would like that—it has some rather nice points. . .' He smiled at the little boy and then addressed Eleanor with unexpected suddenness. 'When do you go back to Edinburgh?'

She looked up from filling second cups. 'In a few days, Friday.'

'Good, I'll drive you down, I've an appointment in that part of the world on Saturday.'

She said stiffly: 'That's kind of you, but I can go very easily by train.'

Her mother looked at her in some astonishment. 'Darling, you've said a dozen times how tedious it is going to Edinburgh by train, and then there's the bus to Lairg first. . .'

'I drive tolerably well,' murmured the doctor. 'We could go to Lairg and on to Inverness. It would save you a good deal of time, but of course, if you are nervous. . .'

'I am not nervous,' said Eleanor coldly. 'I merely do not want to interfere with your holiday.'

'Oh, but you're not,' he told her cheerfully. 'I have to go to Edinburgh—I've just said so. I came here first because I had some books my father wanted your father to have.'

Which led the conversation into quite different channels.

It was a crisp, bright October morning when Eleanor woke the next day—too good to stay in bed, she decided. She got up, moving quietly round her pretty little bedroom, pulling on slacks and a sweater again, brushing and plaiting her hair. She went down to the kitchen without making a sound and put on the kettle; a cup of tea, she decided, then a quick peep at Mrs Trot and the kittens before taking tea up to her parents; and there would still be time to take Punch, the dog, for a short walk before helping to get breakfast.

She was warming the pot when Fulk said from the door: 'Good morning, Eleanor—coming out for a walk? It's a marvellous morning.'

She spooned tea carefully. 'Hullo, have you been out already?'

'Yes, but I'm more than willing to go again. Who's the tea for?'

'Me—and you, now you're here.'

He said softly: 'I wonder why you don't like me, Eleanor?'

She poured tea into two mugs and handed him one, and said seriously:

'I think it's because you arrived unexpectedly—quite out of the blue—you see, I never thought I'd see you again and I didn't like you when I was a little girl. It's funny how one remembers. . .'

He smiled. 'You were such a little girl, but I daresay you were right, I was a horrid boy—most boys are from time to time and you were bad for me; you made me feel like the lord of creation, following me around on those fat legs of yours, staring at me with those eyes, listening to every word I said—your eyes haven't changed at all, Eleanor.'

Her voice was cool. 'How very complimentary you are all of a sudden. You weren't so polite yesterday.'

He strolled over and held out his mug for more tea. 'One sometimes says the wrong thing when one is taken by surprise.'

She didn't bother to think about that; she was pursuing her own train of thought. 'I know I'm big,' she said crossly, 'but I don't need to be reminded of it.'

He looked momentarily surprised and there was a small spark of laughter in his eyes, but all he said was: 'I won't remind you again, I promise. Shall we cry truce and take the dog for a walk? After all, we shall probably not meet again for another twenty years or even longer than that.'

She was aware of disappointment at the very thought. 'All right, but I must just go up to Mother and Father with this tray.'

He was waiting at the kitchen door when she got down again, and Punch was beside him. 'I must take Mrs Trot's breakfast over first,' she warned him.

They crossed the back yard together and rather to her surprise he took the bowl of milk she was carrying from her and mounted the ladder behind her while Punch, wary of Mrs Trot's maternal claws, stayed prudently in the stable. The little cat received them with pleasure, accepted the milk and fish and allowed them to admire her kittens before they left, going down the short lane which separated the manse and the small church from the village. The huddle of houses and cottages was built precariously between the mountains at their back and the sea, tucked almost apologetically into a corner of the rock-encircled sandy bay. As they reached the beach they were met by a chilly wind from the north, dispelling any illusion that the blue sky and sunshine were an aftertaste of summer, so that they were forced to step out briskly, with Punch tearing down to the edge of the sea and then retreating from the cold waves.

Eleanor was surprised to find that she was enjoying Fulk's company; it was obvious, she told herself, that he had grown into an arrogant man, very sure of himself, probably selfish too, even though she had to admit to his charm. All the same, he was proving himself a delightful companion now, talking about everything under the sun in a friendly manner which held no arrogance at all, and when they got back to the house he surprised her still further by laying the breakfast table while she cooked for Margaret before she left for school. Half way through their activities, Henry came down, rather indignant that he had missed the treat of an early morning walk, but more than reconciled to his loss when Fulk offered to take him for a drive in the Panther. The pair of them went away directly after breakfast and weren't seen again until a few minutes before lunch, when they appeared in the kitchen, on excellent terms with each other, and burdened with a large quantity of flowers for Mrs MacFarlane, whisky for the pastor and chocolates for Margaret. And for Eleanor there was a little pink quartz cat, a few inches high and most beautifully carved, sitting very straight and reserved, reminding her very much of Mrs Trot.

'We had the greatest fun,' Henry informed his waiting family, 'and I had an ice cream. We went to the hotel in Tongue—one of those with nuts on top, and the Panther is just super. When I'm grown up I shall have one, too.'

Eleanor, the little cat cradled in her hand, smiled at him lovingly. 'And so you shall, my dear, but now you're going straight up to the bathroom to wash your hands—dinner's ready.'

The rest of the day passed pleasantly enough, and if she had subconsciously hoped that Fulk would suggest another walk, she had no intention of admitting it to herself. As it was, he spent most of the afternoon with his host and after supper they all played cards until the children's bedtime.

She wakened at first light the next morning, to hear her brother's excited whispering under her window, and when she got out of bed to have a look, it was to see him trotting along beside the doctor, laden with fishing paraphernalia—Punch was with them, too; all three of them looked very happy, even from the back.

They came in late for breakfast with a

splendid catch of fish, which provided the main topic of conversation throughout the meal, and when they had finished Mrs MacFarlane said brightly: 'Well, my dears, fish for dinner, provided of course someone will clean it.' A task which Fulk undertook without fuss before driving Mr MacFarlane into Durness to browse over an interesting collection of books an old friend had offered to sell him.

So that Eleanor saw little of their guest until the late afternoon and even then Henry made a cheerful talkative third when they went over to visit Mrs Trot. It was while they were there, sitting on the floor eating apples, that Fulk asked her: 'What time do you leave tomorrow, Eleanor?'

'Well, I don't want to leave at all,' she replied promptly. 'The very thought of hospital nauseates me—I'd like to stay here for ever and ever. . .' She sighed and went on briskly: 'Well, any time after lunch, I suppose. Would two o'clock suit you?'

'Admirably. It's roughly two hundred and fifty miles, isn't it? We should arrive in Edinburgh in good time for dinner—you don't have to be in at any special time, do you?'

'No—no, of course not, but there's no need. . .really I didn't expect. . .that is. . .'

'There's no need to get worked up,' he assured her kindly. 'I shouldn't have asked you if I hadn't wanted to.' He sounded almost brotherly, which made her pleasure at this remark all the more remarkable, although it was quickly squashed when he went on to say blandly: 'I've had no chance to talk to you about Imogen.'

'Oh, well—yes, of course I shall be delighted to hear about her.'

'Who's Imogen?' Henry enquired.

'The lady Fulk is going to marry,' his big sister told him woodenly.

He looked at her with round eyes. 'Then why didn't she come too?'

Fulk answered him good-naturedly, 'She's in the south of France.'

'Why aren't you with her?'

The doctor smiled. 'We seem to have started something, don't we? You see, Henry, Imogen doesn't like this part of Scotland.'

'Why not?' Eleanor beat her brother by a short head with the question.

'She considers it rather remote.'

Eleanor nodded understandingly. 'Well, it is—no shops for sixty miles, no theatres, almost no cinemas and they're miles away too, and high tea instead of dinner in the hotels.'

Fulk turned his head to look at her.

'Exactly so,' he agreed. 'And do you feel like that about it, too, Eleanor?'

She said with instant indignation: 'No, I do not—I love it; I like peace and quiet and nothing in sight but the mountains and the sea and a cottage or two—anyone who feels differently must be very stupid. . .' She opened her eyes wide and put a hand to her mouth. 'Oh, I do beg your pardon—I didn't mean your Imogen.'

'Still the same hasty tongue,' Fulk said mockingly, 'and she isn't my Imogen yet.'

It was fortunate that Henry created a welcome diversion at that moment; wanting to climb a tree or two before teatime, so that the rest of the afternoon was spent doing just that. Fulk, Eleanor discovered, climbed trees very well.

They played cards again until supper time and after their meal, when the two gentlemen retired to the pastor's study, Eleanor declared that she was tired and would go to bed, but once in her room she made no effort to undress but sat on her bed making up her mind what she would wear the next day— Fulk had only seen her in slacks and a sweater with her hair hanging anyhow. She would surprise him.

It was a pity, but he didn't seem in the least surprised. She went down to breakfast looking much as usual, but before lunchtime she changed into a well cut tweed suit of a pleasing russet colour, put on her brogue shoes, made up her pretty face with care, did her hair in a neat, smooth coil on the top of her head, and joined the family at the table. And he didn't say a word, glancing up at her as she entered the room and then looking away again with the careless speed of someone who had seen the same thing a dozen times before. Her excellent appetite was completely destroyed.

It served her right, she told herself severely, for allowing herself to think about him too much; she had no reason to do so, he was of no importance in her life and after today she wasn't likely to see him again. She made light conversation all the way to Tomintoul, a village high in the Highlands, where they stopped for tea. It was a small place, but the hotel overlooked the square and there was plenty to comment upon, something for which she was thankful, for she was becoming somewhat weary of providing almost all the conversation. Indeed, when they were on their way once more and after another hour of commenting upon the scenery, she observed tartly: 'I'm sure you will understand if I don't talk any more; I can't think of anything else to say, and even if I could, I feel I should save it for this evening, otherwise we shall sit at dinner like an old married couple.'

His shoulders shook. 'My dear girl, I had no idea. . . I was enjoying just sitting here and listening to you rambling on—you have a pretty voice, you know.' He paused. 'Imogen doesn't talk much when we drive together; it makes a nice change. But I promise you we won't sit like an old married couple; however old we become, we shall never take each other for granted.'

She allowed this remark to pass without comment, for she wasn't sure what he meant. 'You were going to tell me about Imogen,' she prompted, and was disappointed when he said abruptly: 'I've changed my mind— tell me about Henry instead. What a delightful child he is, but not, I fancy, over-strong.'

The subject of Henry lasted until they reached Edinburgh, where he drove her to the North British Hotel in Princes Street, and after Eleanor had tidied herself, gave her a memorable dinner, managing to convey, without actually saying so, that she was not only a pleasant companion but someone whom he had wanted to take out to dinner all his life. It made her glow very nicely, and the glow was kept at its best by the hock which he offered her. They sat for a long time over their meal and when he at last took her to the hospital it was almost midnight.

She got out of the car at the Nurses' Home entrance and he got out with her and walked to the door to open it. She wished him good-bye quietly, thanked him for a delightful evening and was quite taken by surprise when he pulled her to him, kissed her hard and then, without another word, popped her through the door and closed it behind her. She stood in the dimly lit hall, trying to sort out her feelings. She supposed that they were outraged, but this was tempered by the thought that she wasn't going to see him again. She told herself firmly that it didn't matter in the least, trying to drown the persistent little voice in the back of her head telling her that even if she didn't like him— and she had told herself enough times that she didn't—it mattered quite a bit. She went slowly up to her room, warning herself that just because he had given her a good dinner and been an amusing companion there was no reason to allow her thoughts to dwell upon him.

CHAPTER TWO

THE morning was dark and dreary and suited Eleanor's mood very well as she got into her uniform and, looking the very epitome of neatness and calm efficiency, went down to breakfast, a meal eaten in a hurry by reason of the amount of conversation crammed in by herself and friends while they drank tea and bolted toast and marmalade.

She climbed the stairs to Women's Medical, trying to get used to being back on the ward once more, while her pretty nose registered the fact that the patients had had fish for breakfast and that someone had been too lavish with the floor polish—the two smells didn't go well together. Someone, too, would have to repair the window ledge outside the ward door, and it was obvious that no one had bothered to water the dreadful potted plant which lived on it. Eleanor pushed the swing doors open and went straight to her little office, where Staff Nurse Jill Pitts would be waiting with the two night nurses.

The report took longer than usual; it always did on her first day back, even if she had been away for a short time; new patients, new treatments, Path Lab reports, news of old patients—it was all of fifteen minutes before she sent the night nurses to their breakfast, left Jill to see that the nurses were starting on their various jobs, and set off on her round. She spent some time with her first three patients, for they were elderly and ill, and for some weeks now they had all been battling to keep them alive; she assured herself that they were holding their own and passed on to the fourth bed; Mrs McFinn, a large, comfortable lady with a beaming smile and a regrettable shortness of breath due to asthma, a condition which didn't prevent her wheezing out a little chat with Eleanor, and her neighbour, puffing and panting her way through emphysema with unending courage and good humour, wanted to chat too. She indulged them both; they were such dears, but so for that matter were almost all the patients in the ward.

She spent a few minutes with each of them in turn, summing up their condition while she lent a friendly ear and a smile; only as she reached the top of the ward did she allow a small sigh to escape her. Miss Tremble, next in line, was a cross the entire staff, medical and nursing, bore with fortitude, even if a good deal of grumbling went on about her in private. She was a thin, acidulated woman in her sixties, a diabetic which it seemed impossible to stabilize however the doctors tried. Painstakingly dieted and injected until the required balance had been reached, she would be sent home, only to be borne back in again sooner or later in yet another diabetic coma, a condition which she never ceased to blame upon the hospital staff. She had been in again for two weeks now, and on the one occasion during that period when it had been considered safe to send her home again to her downtrodden sister, she had gone into a coma again as she was actually on the point of departure, and it was all very well for Sir Arthur Minch, the consultant physician in charge of her case, to carry on about it; as Eleanor had pointed out to him in a reasonable manner, one simply didn't turn one's back on hyperglycaemia, even when it was about to leave the ward; she had put the patient back to bed again and allowed the great man to natter on about wanting the bed for an urgent case. He had frowned and tutted and in the end had agreed with her; she had known that he would, anyway.

She took up her position now at the side of Miss Tremble's bed and prepared to listen to its occupant's long list of complaints; she had heard them many times before, and would most likely hear them many more times in the future. She put on her listening face and thought about Fulk, wondering where he was and why he had come to Edinburgh. She would have liked to have asked him, only she had hesitated; he had a nasty caustic tongue, she remembered it vividly when he had stayed with them all those years ago, and she had no doubt that he still possessed it. She could only guess— he could of course be visiting friends, or perhaps he had come over to consult with a colleague; he might even have a patient. . . She frowned and Miss Tremble said irritably: 'I'm glad to see that you are annoyed, Sister—it is disgraceful that I had to have Bovril on two successive evenings when my appetite needs tempting.'

Eleanor made a soothing reply, extolled the virtues of the despised beverage, assured Miss Tremble that something different would be offered her for her supper that evening, and moved on to the next bed, but even when she had completed her round and was back in her office, immersed in forms, charts and the answering of the constantly ringing telephone she was still wondering about Fulk.

But presently she gave herself a mental shake; she would never know anyway. Thinking about him was a complete waste of time, especially with Sir Arthur due to do his round at ten o'clock. She pushed the papers to one side with a touch of impatience; they would have to wait until she had checked the ward and made sure that everything was exactly as it should be for one of the major events in the ward's week.

She ran the ward well; the patients were ready with five minutes to spare and the nurses were going, two by two, to their coffee break. Eleanor, longing for a cup herself, but having to wait for it until Sir Arthur should be finished, was in the ward, with the faithful Jill beside her and Mrs MacDonnell, the part-time staff nurse, hovering discreetly with a student nurse close by to fetch and carry. She knew Sir Arthur's ways well by now; he would walk into the ward at ten o'clock precisely with his registrar, his house doctor and such students as had the honour of accompanying him that morning. Eleanor, with brothers of her own, felt a sisterly concern for the shy ones, whose wits invariably deserted them the moment they entered the ward, and she had formed the habit of stationing herself where she might prompt those rendered dumb by apprehension when their chief chose to fire a question at them. She had become something of an expert at mouthing clues helpful enough to start the hapless recipient of Sir Arthur's attention on the path of a right answer. Perhaps one day she would be caught red-handed, but in the meantime she continued to pass on vital snippets to any number of grateful young gentlemen.

The clock across the square had begun its sonorous rendering of the hour when the ward doors swung open just as usual and the senior Medical Consultant, his posse of attendants hard on his heels, came in—only it wasn't quite as usual; Fulk van Hensum was walking beside him, not the Fulk of the last day or so, going fishing with Henry in an outsize sweater and rubber boots, or playing Canasta with the family after supper or good-naturedly helping Margaret with her decimals. This was a side of him which she hadn't seen before; he looked older for a start, and if anything, handsomer in a distinguished way, and his face wore the expression she had seen so often on a doctor's face; calm and kind and totally unflappable—and a little remote. He was also impeccably turned out, his grey suit tailored to perfection, his tie an elegant understatement. She advanced to meet them, very composed, acknowledging Sir Arthur's stately greeting with just the right degree of warmth and turning a frosty eye on Fulk, who met it blandly with the faintest of smiles and an equally bland: 'Good morning, Eleanor, how nice to be able to surprise you twice in only a few days.'

She looked down her nose at him. 'Good morning, Doctor van Hensum,' she greeted him repressively, and didn't smile. He might have told her; there had been no reason at all why he shouldn't have done so. She almost choked when he went on coolly: 'Yes, I could have told you, couldn't I? But you never asked me.'

Sir Arthur glanced at Eleanor. 'Know each other, do you?' he wanted to know genially.

Before she could answer, Fulk observed pleasantly: 'Oh, yes—for many years. Eleanor was almost five when we first met.' He had the gall to smile at her in what she considered to be a patronising manner.

'Five, eh?' chuckled Sir Arthur. 'Well, you've grown since then, Sister.' The chuckle became a laugh at his little joke and she managed to smile too, but with an effort for Fulk said: 'She had a quantity of long hair and she was very plump.' He stared at her and she frowned fiercely. 'Little girls are rather sweet,' his voice was silky, 'but they tend to change as they grow up.'

She all but ground her teeth at him; it was a relief when Sir Arthur said cheerfully: 'Well, well, I suppose we should get started, Sister.

Doctor van Hensum is particularly interested in that case of agranulocytosis—Mrs Lee, isn't it? She experienced the first symptoms while she was on holiday in Holland and came under his care. Most fortunately for her, he diagnosed it at once—a difficult thing to do.' His eye swept round the little group of students, who looked suitably impressed.

'Not so very difficult in this case, if I might say so,' interpolated Fulk quietly. 'There was the typical sore throat and oedema, and the patient answered my questions with great intelligence. . .'

'But no doubt the questions were intelligent,' remarked Sir Arthur dryly, and the students murmured their admiration, half of them not having the least idea what their superiors were talking about, anyway.

They were moving towards the first bed now, and Eleanor, casting a quick look at Fulk, saw that he had become the consultant again; indeed, as the round progressed, his manner towards her was faultless; politely friendly, faintly impersonal—they could have just met for the first time. It vexed her to find that this annoyed her more than his half-teasing attitude towards her when he had entered the ward. He was a tiresome man, she decided, leading the way to Mrs Lee's bed.

That lady was making good progress now

that she was responding to the massive doses of penicillin, and although her temperature was still high and she remained lethargic, she was certainly on the mend. Sir Arthur held forth at some length, occasionally pausing to verify some point with the Dutch doctor and then firing questions at random at whichever unfortunate student happened to catch his eye. Most of them did very well, but one or two of them were tongue-tied by the occasion. Eleanor, unobtrusively helping out one such, and standing slightly behind Sir Arthur, had just finished miming the bare bones of the required information when she realized that Fulk had moved and was standing where he could watch her. She threw him a frowning glance which he appeared not to see, for the smile he gave her was so charming that she only just prevented herself from smiling back at him.

Perhaps he wasn't so bad after all, she conceded, only to have this opinion reversed when, the round over, she was bidding Sir Arthur and his party goodbye at the ward door, for when she bade Fulk goodbye too, he said at once: 'You'll lunch with me, Eleanor,' and it wasn't even a question, let alone a request, delivered in a silky voice loud enough for everyone to hear.

'I'm afraid that's impossible,' she began

coldly, and Sir Arthur, quite mistaking her hesitation, interrupted her to say heartily: 'Nonsense, of course you can go, Sister—I've seen you dozens of times at the Blue Bird Café'—an establishment much favoured by the hospital staff because it was only just down the road and they were allowed to go there in uniform—'Why, only a couple of weeks ago you were having a meal there with young Maddox, although how he managed that when he was on call for the Accident Room I cannot imagine.'

He turned his attention to Fulk. 'The Blue Bird isn't exactly Cordon Bleu, but they do a nice plate of fish and chips, and there is the great advantage of being served quickly.' He looked at Eleanor once more. 'You intended going to your dinner, I suppose? When do you go?'

She didn't want to answer, but she had to say something. 'One o'clock,' she told him woodenly and heard his pleased: 'Excellent—what could be better? Van Hensum, we shall have time to talk over that case we were discussing.' He beamed in a fatherly fashion at Eleanor, fuming silently, and led the way down the corridor with all the appearance of a man who had done someone a good turn and felt pleased about it. Fulk went with him, without saying another word.

Eleanor snorted, muttered rudely under her breath and went to serve the patients' dinners, and as she dished out boiled fish, nourishing stew, fat-free diets, high-calorie diets and diabetic diets, she pondered how she could get out of having lunch with Fulk. She wasn't quite sure why it was so important that she should escape going with him, because actually she liked the idea very much, and even when, as usual, she was battling with Miss Tremble about the amount of ham on her plate, a small part of her brain was still hard at work trying to discover the reason. All the same, she told herself that her determination not to go was strong enough to enable her to make some excuse.

She was trying to think of one as she went back to her office with Jill, to give her a brief run-down of jobs to be done during the next hour—a waste of time, as it turned out, for Fulk was there, standing idly looking out of the window. He had assumed his consultant's manner once more, too, so that Eleanor found it difficult to utter the refusal she had determined upon. Besides, Jill was there, taking it for granted that she was going, even at that very moment urging her not to hurry back. 'There's nothing much on this afternoon,' she pointed out, 'not until three o'clock at any rate, and you never get your full hour for dinner, Sister.' She made a face. 'It's braised heart, too.'

Fulk's handsome features expressed extreme distaste. 'How revolting,' he observed strongly. 'Eleanor, put on your bonnet at once and we will investigate the fish and chips. They sound infinitely more appetizing.'

Eleanor dabbed with unusually clumsy fingers at the muslin trifle perched on her great knot of shining hair. 'Thanks, Jill, I'll see.' She sounded so reluctant that her right hand looked at her in amazement while Fulk's eyes gleamed with amusement, although all he said was: 'Shall we go?'

The café was almost full, a number of hospital staff, either on the point of going on duty or just off, were treating themselves to egg and chips, spaghetti on toast or the fish and chips for which the café was justly famous. Fulk led the way to a table in the centre of the little place, and Eleanor, casting off her cloak and looking around, nodded and smiled at two physiotherapists, an X-ray technician, and the senior Accident Room Sister with the Casualty Officer. There were two of the students who had been in Sir Arthur's round that morning sitting at the next table and they smiled widely at her, glanced at Fulk and gave her the thumbs-up sign, which she pointedly ignored, hoping that her companion hadn't seen it too. He had; he said: 'Lord, sometimes I feel middle-aged.'

'Well,' her voice was astringent, 'you're not—you're not even married yet.'

His mouth twitched. 'You imply that being married induces middle age, and that's nonsense.' He added slowly: 'I imagine that any man who married you would tend to regain his youth, not lose it.'

She gaped at him across the little table. 'For heaven's sake, whatever makes you say that?' But she wasn't to know, for the proprietor of the Blue Bird had made his way towards them and was offering a menu card. He was a short, fat man and rather surprisingly, a Cockney; the soul of kindness and not above allowing second helpings for free to anyone who was a bit short until pay day. He stood looking at them both now and then said: ''Ullo, Sister, 'aven't met yer friend before, 'ave I?'

'No, Steve—he's a Dutch consultant, a friend of Sir Arthur Minch. Doctor van Hensum, this is Steve who runs the café.'

The doctor held out a hand and Steve shook it with faint surprise. 'Pleased ter meet yer,' he pronounced in gratified tones. 'I got a nice bit of 'ake out the back. 'Ow'd yer like it, the pair of yer? Chips and peas and a good cuppa while yer waiting.'

A cheerful girl brought the tea almost at once and Eleanor poured the rich brew into the thick cups and handed one to Fulk. 'Aren't you sorry you asked me out now?' she wanted to know. 'I don't suppose you've ever had your lunch in a place like this before.'

He gave her a thoughtful look. 'You're determined to make me out a very unpleasant fellow, aren't you? I wonder why?' He passed her the sugar bowl and then helped himself. 'No, I've never been in a place quite like this one before, but I've been in far worse, and let me tell you, my girl, that your low opinion of me is completely mistaken.'

'I never. . .' began Eleanor, and was interrupted by the arrival of the hake, mouth-watering in its thick rich batter coat and surrounded by chips and peas; by the time they had assured Steve that it looked delicious, passed each other the salt, refused the vinegar and refilled their cups, there seemed no point in arguing. They fell to and what conversation there was was casual and good-humoured. Presently, nicely mellowed by the food, Eleanor remarked: 'You were going to tell me about Imogen.'

He selected a chip with deliberation and

ate it slowly. 'Not here,' he told her.

'You keep saying that—you said it in the car yesterday. Do you have to have soft music and stained glass windows or something before she can be talked about?'

He put his head on one side and studied her face. 'You're a very rude girl—I suppose that's what comes of being a bossy elder sister. No, perhaps that's too sweeping a statement,' he continued blandly, 'for Henry assured me that you were the grooviest—I'm a little vague as to the exact meaning of the word, but presumably it is a compliment of the highest order.'

'Bless the boy, it is.' She hesitated. 'I'd like to thank you for being so kind to him— he's a poppet, at least we all think so, and far too clever for his age, though he's a great one for adventure; he's for ever falling out of trees and going on long solitary walks with Punch and tumbling off rocks into the sea when he goes fishing. We all long to tell him not to do these things, but he's a boy. . . having you for a companion was bliss for him.'

'And would it have been bliss for you, Eleanor?' Fulk asked in an interested voice, and then: 'No, don't answer, I can see the words blistering your lips. We'll go on talking about Henry—he's not quite as strong as you would like, your father tells me.'

She had decided to overlook the first part of his remark. 'He's tough, it's just that he catches everything that's going; measles, whooping cough, mumps, chickenpox—you name it, he's had it.'

He passed his cup for more tea, eyed its rich brown strength, sugared it lavishly and took a sip with an expressionless face. 'I shudder to think what this tea is doing to our insides,' he remarked lightly. 'Have you a good doctor?'

'Doctor MacClew. He's quite old now, but he's been our doctor all our lives. He's a dear and so kind, although I daresay he's old-fashioned by your standards.'

'My standards?' He looked quite shocked. 'My dear Eleanor, you're at it again, turning me into someone I'm not. Why should you suppose that I would set myself up above another doctor, probably twice my age and with at least twice my experience, and who has had to improvise, make decisions, take risks, diagnose without X-rays and be his own Path Lab in an emergency? I, remember, have the whole range of modern equipment and science behind me—I need not open my mouth until all the answers have been given me.'

She said indignantly: 'Don't exaggerate.

That's not true; a good physician doesn't need any of those things—they only confirm his opinion. You know as well as I do that you could manage very well without them.'

He lifted his thick brows in mock surprise. 'Why, Eleanor, those are the first kind words you have uttered since we met.' He grinned so disarmingly that she smiled back at him. 'Well, you know it's true.'

He said slowly, watching her: 'Do you know I believe that's the first time you've smiled at me? Oh, you've gone through the motions, but they didn't register. You should smile more often.' He heaved a sigh. 'How delightful it is not to be quarrelling with you.'

She eyed him with disfavour. 'What a beastly thing to say! I've not quarrelled with you, I've been very polite.'

'I know, I'd rather quarrel, but not now—let's call a truce.'

She seized her opportunity. 'Tell me about Imogen.'

He leaned back on the hard wooden chair. 'What do you want to know?'

Eleanor was so surprised at his meek acceptance of her question that she didn't speak for a moment. 'Well, what does she do and where does she live and where will you live when you're married, and is she very pretty?' She added wistfully: 'You said she was small. . .'

'Half your size and very, very pretty—you forgot to ask how old she is, by the way. Twenty-six, and she doesn't do anything— at least, she doesn't have a job. She doesn't need to work, you see. But she fills her days very nicely with tennis and swimming and riding and driving—and she dances beauti- fully. She lives in den Haag and I live near Groningen, about a hundred and fifty miles apart—an easy run on the motorway.'

'But that's an awful long way to go each weekend,' observed Eleanor.

'Every weekend? Oh, not as often as that, my dear. Besides, Imogen stays with friends a good deal—I did tell you that she's in the south of France now and later on she will be going to Switzerland for the winter sports.' His voice was very level. 'We decided when we became engaged that we would make no claims on each other's time and leisure.'

'Oh,' said Eleanor blankly, 'how very strange. I don't think I'd like that at all.'

'If you were engaged to me? But you're not.' He smiled thinly. 'A fine state of affairs that would be! You would probably expect me to sit in your pocket and we should quarrel without pause.'

'Probably.' Her voice was colourless. 'I

think I'd better go back to the ward, if you don't mind. . .' She was interrupted by the cheerful booming voice of Doctor Blake, Sir Arthur's right-hand man, who clapped a hand on her shoulder, greeted her with the easy friendliness of a long-standing acquaintance and asked: 'May I sit down? It's Doctor van Hensum, isn't it? I've just been with Sir Arthur and he mentioned that you might be here still—I'm not interrupting anything, am I?'

'I'm just on my way back to the ward,' said Eleanor, and wished she wasn't. 'I'm a bit late already.' She smiled a general sort of smile and got to her feet. 'Thanks for the lunch,' she said quickly and hardly looking at Fulk. He had got to his feet too, and his 'Goodbye, Eleanor,' was very quiet.

She had no time to think about him after that, for Miss Tremble had seen fit to go into a coma and it took most of the afternoon to get her out of it again. Eleanor missed her tea and the pleasant half hour of gossip she usually enjoyed with the other Sisters and went off duty a little late, to change rapidly and catch a bus to the other side of the city where an aunt, elderly, crotchety but nevertheless one of the family, would be waiting to give her supper. It had become a custom for Eleanor to visit her on her return from any holidays so that she might supply her with any titbits of news, and although it was sometimes a little tiresome, the old lady had got to depend upon her visits. She spent a dull evening, answering questions and listening to her companion's various ailments, and when she at last escaped and returned to the hospital, she was too tired to do more than climb into bed as quickly as possible.

It was two more days before she discovered, quite by chance, that Fulk had gone back to Holland only a few hours after they had shared their meal together in the Blue Bird Café, and for some reason the news annoyed her; she had been wondering about him, it was true, but somehow she had taken it for granted that he would come and say goodbye before he left, although there was no reason why he should have done so, but one would have thought, she told herself peevishly, that after making such a thing about taking her to lunch, he could at least have mentioned that he was on the point of leaving; he hadn't even said goodbye. She paused in her reflections: he had, even though he hadn't told her he was leaving; probably thinking it was none of her business, anyway—nor was it.

She glared at her nice face in the silly little mirror on the office wall and went back to

her work once more, and while she chatted
with her patients and listened to their complaints and worries, she decided that Fulk
wasn't worth thinking about, quite forgetting
that she had told herself that already. She
would most probably not see him again; she
could forget him, and the beautiful Imogen
with him. She finished her round and went
back down the ward, the very picture of calm
efficiency, and went into her office, where
she sat at her desk, staring at the papers she
was supposed to be dealing with while she
speculated about Imogen; it was strange that
although she had never met the girl and was
never likely to, she should have such strong
feelings of dislike for her.

CHAPTER THREE

THE days slid by, October became November and the bright weather showed no sign of giving way to the sleet and gales of early winter. The ward filled up; acute bronchitis, pneumonia, 'flu in a variety of forms, followed each other with an almost monotonous regularity. Eleanor, brimming over with good health and vitality herself, had her kind heart wrung by every fresh case. They got well again, of course, at least the vast majority did, what with antibiotics and skilled nursing and Sir Arthur and his assistants keeping a constant eye upon them all, but Eleanor, wrapping some elderly lady in a shabby winter coat, preparatory to her going home, wished with all her heart that they might stay in the ward, eating the plain wholesome food they never cooked for themselves, enjoying the warmth and the company of other elderly ladies; instead of which, going home so often meant nothing more than a chilly, lonely bed-sitter.

They weren't all elderly, though. There was the teenager, who should have been

49

pretty and lively and nicely curved, but who had succumbed to the craze for slimming and had been so unwise about it that now she was a victim of anorexia nervosa; the very sight of food had become repugnant to her, and although she was nothing but skin and bone, she still wanted to become even slimmer. Eleanor had a hard time with her, but it was rewarding after a week or two to know that she had won and once again her patient could be persuaded to eat. And the diabetics, of course, nothing as dramatic as Miss Tremble, but short-stay patients who came in to be stabilized, and lastly, the heart patients; the dramatic coronaries who came in with such urgency and needed so much care, and the less spectacular forms of heart disease, who nonetheless received just as much attention. Eleanor didn't grudge her time or her energy on her patients; off-duty didn't matter, and when Jill remonstrated with her she said carelessly that she could give herself a few extra days later on, when the ward was slack.

And towards the end of November things did calm down a bit, and Eleanor, a little tired despite her denials, decided that she might have a long weekend at home. She left the hospital after lunch on Friday and took the long train journey to Lairg and then the bus to Tongue, warmly wrapped against the weather in her tweed coat and little fur hat her mother had given her for the previous Christmas, and armed with a good book, and because it was a long journey, she took a thermos of tea and some sandwiches as well. All the same, despite these precautions, she was tired and hungry by the time she reached the Manse, but her welcome was warm and the supper her mother had waiting was warm and filling as well. She ate and talked at the same time and then went up to bed. It was heavenly to be home again; the peace and quiet of it were a delight after the busy hospital life. She curled up in her narrow little bed and went instantly to sleep.

She was up early, though, ready to help with the breakfast and see Margaret and Henry off to school, and then go and visit Mrs Trot and her fast-growing family. 'We'll have to find homes for them,' she declared as she helped with the washing up.

'Yes, dear.' Mrs MacFarlane emptied her bowl and dried her hands. 'We have—for two of them, and we thought we'd keep one—company for Mrs Trot, she's such a good mother—that leaves one.'

'Oh, good.' Eleanor was stacking plates on the old-fashioned wooden dresser. 'What's all this about Henry going climbing?'

'His class is going this afternoon, up to that cairn—you know the one? It's about two miles away, isn't it? Mr MacDow is going with them, of course, and it's splendid weather with a good forecast. He's promised that they'll explore those caves nearby.'

'The whole class? That'll be a dozen or more, I don't envy him.'

Mrs MacFarlane laughed. 'He's very competent, you know, and a first-class climber—the boys adore him.' She looked a little anxious. 'Do you suppose that Henry shouldn't have gone?'

'Oh, Mother, no. Can you imagine how he would feel if he were left behind? Besides, he's pretty good on his own, remember, and he knows the country almost as well as I do.'

Her mother looked relieved. 'Yes, that's true,' she smiled. 'I've always said that if I got lost on the mountains I wouldn't be at all frightened if I knew you were searching for me.'

Eleanor gave her mother a daughterly hug. 'Let's get on with the dinner, then at least Henry can start out on a full stomach. Are they to be back for tea? It gets dark early. . .'

'Five o'clock at the latest, Mr MacDow said—they'll have torches with them. . .I thought we'd have treacle scones and I baked a cake yesterday—he'll be hungry.'

Henry, well fed, suitably clothed, and admonished by his three elder relations to mind what the teacher said and not to go off by himself, was seen off just after one o'clock. The afternoon was fine, with the sky still blue and the cold sunshine lighting up the mountains he was so eager to climb. Not that there was anything hazardous about the expedition; they would follow the road, a narrow one full of hairpin bends, until they reached the cairn in the dip between the mountains encircling it, and then, if there was time, they would explore the caves.

'I shall probably find something very exciting,' said Henry importantly as he set off on his short walk back to the village school where they were to foregather.

Eleanor stood at the door and watched them set out, waving cheerfully to Mr MacDow, striding behind the boys like a competent shepherd with a flock of sheep. She said out loud: 'I'd better make some chocolate buns as well,' and sniffed the air as she turned to go indoors again; it had become a good deal colder.

She didn't notice at first that it was becoming dark far too early; her mother was having a nap in the sitting room, her father would be writing his sermon in his study and she had been fully occupied in the kitchen, but now she went to the window and looked out. The blue sky had become grey, and looking towards the sea she saw that it had become a menacing grey, lighted by a pale yellowish veil hanging above it. 'Snow,' she said, and her voice sounded urgent in the quiet kitchen and even as she spoke the window rattled with violence of a sudden gust of wind. It was coming fast too; the sea, grey and turbulent, was already partly blotted out. She hurried out of the kitchen and into the sitting room and found her mother still sleeping, and when she went into the study it was to find her father dozing too. She took another look out of the window and saw the first slow snowflakes falling; a blizzard was on the way, coming at them without warning. She prayed that Mr MacDow had seen it too and was already on the way down the mountain with the boys. She remembered then that if they had already reached the cairn, there would be no view of the sea from it, the mountains around them would cut off everything but the sky above them. She went back to her father and roused him gently. 'There's a blizzard on the way,' she told him urgently. 'What ought we to do? The boys. . .'

The pastor was instantly alert. 'The time,' he said at once. 'What is the time, my dear?'

She glanced at the clock on the old-fashioned mantelpiece. 'Just after three o'clock.'

'MacDow gave me some sort of time-table—he usually does, you know, so that we have some idea. . .if I remember rightly, they were to have reached the cairn by half past two. He intended to give them a short talk there; interesting geographical features and so on, and between a quarter to three and the hour they would enter the caves and remain there until half past three. They're simple caves, nothing dangerous, and it's possible they're still inside them, unaware of the weather conditions. He's sensible enough to remain in them until the weather clears—it's probably only a brief storm.'

He got up and went to look from the window in his turn. The snow was coming down in good earnest now and the wind had risen, howling eerily round the little house. 'I'm afraid,' said the pastor, 'that this is no brief storm. With this wind there'll be drifts and the road will be blocked and there's no visibility. . . We'd better get a search party organised.' He looked worried. 'It's a pity that almost all the men are at work. . .'

'I'll wake Mother,' Eleanor told him, 'while you ring Mr Wallace.' She sped back into the sitting room, roused her mother, and went back into the hall to get her boots and anorak; she would be going with Mr Wallace, the owner of the only garage within miles, and any other man available, she hadn't been boasting when she had said that she knew the surrounding country like the back of her hand, even in the worst weather she had a natural instinct for direction. She was tugging on her boots when someone rang the front door bell and she called: 'Come in, the door's open.' It would be someone from the village come to consult the pastor about the dangers of the weather.

It wasn't anyone from the village; it was Fulk, standing there, shaking the snow from his shoulders. 'Hullo, everyone,' he said cheerfully, just as though he had seen them only an hour or so previously, 'what filthy weather,' and then: 'What's wrong?'

They were all in the hall now and it was Mrs MacFarlane who explained: 'The children—Henry's class at school—they went up the mountain for a geographical climb—more than a dozen of them with Mr MacDow, their teacher. They're all properly clothed and equipped, but this weather—there was no warning—it's a freak blizzard; it could last for hours and it's not very safe up there in bad weather.' Her voice faltered a little.

His voice was very calm. 'A dozen or more boys—is Henry with them?'

The pastor nodded. 'We were just deciding what's the best thing to do—there are very few men in the village at this time of day. . .'

He paused and Mrs MacFarlane said suddenly: 'It's wonderful to see you, Fulk.'

Eleanor hadn't said a word. Relief at the sight of Fulk had given way to the certainty that now everything would be all right; he looked dependable, sure of himself and quite unworried, whatever his hidden feelings might be; probably it was his very bulk which engendered such a strong feeling of confidence in him, but it was a pleasant sensation, like handing someone else a heavy parcel to carry.

'How far up?' he asked, and looked at her.

'There's a cleft in the mountains about two miles up—it's on the right of the road and there's a cairn. . .it's sheltered on all sides and there are caves quite close by. They were going to explore them.'

She looked out of the window again. The howling gale and the snow were, if anything, rather worse.

'The road?'

'Narrow—about one in six, perhaps more in some places, and there are three hairpin bends.'

He said nothing for a moment and then grinned suddenly, reminding her very much of Henry when he was plotting something. 'Is there a bus in the village?'

She understood at once. 'Yes, Mr Wallace has one, a fourteen-seater, old but reliable—he's got chains too.'

'Good. We'll want rope, torches, blankets—you know all that better than I do—whisky too, shovels and some sacks.'

'How many men will you take?' asked the pastor. 'There aren't many to choose from, I'm afraid: old MacNab and Mr Wallace, and myself, of course.'

'One with me—if we make a mess of it, a search party can start out on foot. Give us an hour.'

'I'm coming with you,' Eleanor said quietly.

Fulk didn't seem surprised. 'I thought you might. I'm going to see about borrowing that bus—could you get some tea in flasks to take with us?'

Eleanor was already on the way to the kitchen. 'I'll see to it. How did you come?'

'With the Panther. I drove straight into the stable—I hope that's all right?' He nodded cheerfully to all three of them as he opened the door, letting in a flurry of snow and a powerful gust of wind before shutting it behind him.

He was back in a surprisingly short time,

the lights of the bus lightening the snowy gloom as he came to a slithering halt before the door. He got out, leaving the engine running, and came indoors bringing Mr Wallace with him.

'Ye'll need a man who kens the road,' remarked that gentleman once they were inside. They stamped the snow off their boots and shook their shoulders, making havoc in Mrs MacFarlane's neat hall.

'Well,' said Fulk, 'Eleanor said she would come—she knows the way.' He smiled at Mr Wallace with great charm. 'I should value your advice on this—it seems a fairly sensible idea, for if we make a mess of things you would be here to organize a search party on foot, something I wouldn't know a thing about. I understand the men are away from home until the evening.'

Mr Wallace nodded. 'Building an extension on the hotel in Tongue, though they'll not get far in this, neither will they get home all that easy.' He gave a not unfriendly grunt. 'Ye're a good driver? My bus isn't any of your fancy cars, ye ken.'

'I've taken part in a number of rallies,' murmured Fulk, and left it at that, and Mr Wallace grunted again. 'We'll need to clear the school house—aye, and get blankets too.'

Fulk nodded. 'Are there enough men to

mount a search if necessary?'

'Aye,' said Mr Wallace again, 'we'll manage. Ye'd best be off.'

Fulk turned to look at Eleanor standing patiently, muffled in her hooded anorak, slacks stuffed into boots, a woollen scarf tugged tight round her throat and a pair of woollen mitts on her hands. 'OK?' he asked, and didn't wait for her answer. 'We'll be back as soon as possible,' he assured her parents. 'Give us a couple of hours, won't you?'

He bent to kiss Mrs MacFarlane on the cheek, swept Eleanor before him out of the house and opened the bus door for her. 'Thank God you're a great strapping girl,' he observed as he climbed into the driver's seat beside her, 'for I fancy we shall have to do a good deal of shovelling on the way.'

Eleanor said 'Probably,' in a cold voice; until that moment she had been more than glad to see him, now she wasn't so sure. Even in the most awkward of situations no girl likes to be described as strapping.

They didn't speak again for a little while; Fulk was occupied in keeping the bus on the road down to the village and then out on the other side, away from the sea towards the mountains. The snow was falling fast now, tossed in all directions by the violence of the wind. The road had disappeared too, although the telegraph wires were a guide until they reached the side road which would take them up between the mountains.

Fulk braked gently. 'Up here?' and Eleanor, staring ahead at the little she could see, said: 'Yes—we must be mad.'

Her companion laughed. 'Though this be madness, yet there is method in't—and that's your Shakespeare, and a very sensible remark too.' He changed gear and started up the narrow road.

They were soon in trouble; the first bend came after a hundred yards or so, and although it wasn't a sharp one and it was still possible to see its curve, the bus skidded on the bank of snow which had already built up along its edge. Fulk prepared to get out. 'Keep the engine going, whatever you do,' he cautioned her, and disappeared into the swirling snow, armed with sacks and shovel. It seemed an age before he climbed in again, the snow thick on him. Eleanor slid back into her own seat and brushed him down as best she could, then sat tensely while he hauled the bus round the bend. It went with reluctance, sliding and slipping, but the sacks held the back wheels and they were round at last.

'I don't dare to stop now,' said Fulk. 'The sacks will have to stay—is it straight ahead?'

'Yes—there's a spiky rock on the left before the next bend, it's a sharp one and there's bound to be a drift—I should think we'll both have to dig.'

He spared a brief, smiling glance. 'OK, if you say so—it'll mean leaving the bus, though.' He began to whistle, and she realized that he was enjoying himself, and upon reflection she was bound to admit that so was she, in a scary kind of way.

It took them ten minutes' hard digging to clear the angle of the road when they reached it. Eleanor had got out when she saw the rock, and floundered ahead in the appalling weather, looking for landmarks—a stunted tree, the vague outline of the railing which guarded the angle of the road. Once she was sure of them she waved to Fulk, who joined her with the shovels, leaving the bus reluctantly ticking over. They worked together until they had made some sort of track, so that Fulk, with a great deal of skill and muttered bad language, was able to go on again, toiling up the road, narrower and steeper now but happily sheltered a little on one side from the gale, so that although there were great drifts piling up on the opposite bank, their side of the road was still fairly clear.

Eleanor blew on her cold fingers. 'We're nearly half way—there's a left-hand bend in about fifty yards—very exposed, I'm afraid.'

Fulk chuckled. 'Eleanor, if ever I should need to go to the North Pole, remind me to take you with me; you seem to have an instinctive sense of direction.' He had raised his voice to a shout, for the wind, now that they were higher, was howling round the bus, beating on its windows, driving the snow in thick, crazily spiralling flurries.

Eleanor wiped the windscreen uselessly. 'It's somewhere here,' she cried, and as the windscreen wipers cleared the view for a few seconds: 'You can just see the beginning of the curve—there's a stone. . .it's blocked further on,' she added rather unnecessarily.

'Work to do, girl,' said Fulk cheerfully, 'and for heaven's sake don't go wandering off; I'd never find you again. Out you get, I'll fetch the shovels.'

It was hard work, even clearing a rough path just wide enough for the bus was an agonisingly laborious business. Eleanor, shovelling away with her young strong arms, found herself wondering how her companion's Imogen would have fared. Would she have shovelled? Would she have come on the crazy trip in the first place? Decidedly not; she would have stayed behind by the fire, and when Fulk returned she would have greeted him with girlish charm, deliciously

scented and gowned, and with not a hair out
of place, and he would have called her his
precious darling, or something equally silly.
Eleanor, her spleen nicely stirred, shovelled
even harder.

It was heaven to get back into the bus at
last. She sat, huffing and puffing in its warm
haven, looking like a snowman. Fulk, getting
in beside her, looked her over carefully.
'Cold but cuddly,' he pronounced, and
leaned over to kiss her surprised mouth.
Heaven knew what she might have said to
that, but he gave her no chance to speak,
starting at once on the slow business of coax-
ing the bus along the road once more, an
operation fraught with such difficulties that
she was kept fully occupied peering ahead,
ready to warn him should he get too near to
the low stone wall, just visible, guarding the
outer edge of the road. The other side was
shut in now by towering rocks, which, while
forbidding, at least served as a guide.

'The cairn's on the right,' declared
Eleanor, 'where the rock stops, and for
heaven's sake be careful, there's a kind of
canyon, fairly level once you get into it. If
they're sheltering anywhere near, they must
surely see our lights.'

Fulk didn't answer. He was fully occupied
in keeping the bus steady; it took several

attempts to get round the rocks and into the canyon, for the bus danced and skidded as though its wheels were legs, but once they were between the walls of rock, it was comparatively peaceful—true, the wind howled like a banshee and the snow was as thick as ever, but there was a semblance of shelter. Fulk skidded to a slow halt, leaving the engine running. 'Journey's end,' he declared. 'Now to find everyone and stow them away before we die of exposure.'

They got out and stood, holding hands for safety's sake, striving to pierce the gloom around them. 'Someone's shouting,' cried Eleanor, 'and there's a torch—look, over there, to our right,' and when she would have started off, found herself held firmly against Fulk.

'No, wait—stay just where you are while I get the rope.'

She hadn't thought of that in the excitement and relief of knowing that the boys were safe and found; she waited patiently while he secured the rope to the bus and paid out a length of it, slinging the coils over one arm. 'Now we can all get back,' he pointed out, and took her by the arm. 'Switch on your torch, the more light the better.'

The boys were all together, close against an overhanging rock which afforded them some shelter, and when they would have plunged forward to meet them, Fulk shouted: 'Stay where you are—where's Mr MacDow?'

It was Henry who shouted back. 'He's here, behind us, Fulk—he's hurt his leg. He fell down outside the cave and now he doesn't answer us any more.'

Eleanor heard Fulk mutter something, then shout: 'Is there anyone in the caves still?'

There was a chorus of 'No's and a babble of voices explaining that when they had wanted to leave the caves the entrance had been almost completely blocked with snow. 'We had to dig with our hands,' explained Henry, and then: 'Can we go home now—it's cold.'

Fulk was tying the rope round himself. 'This minute,' he bellowed hearteningly. 'Eleanor, I'll stay here and have a look at MacDow, get this lot collected up and hustle them into the bus and make sure that every one of them has a hand on the rope—Understood?'

She heard herself say in a meek voice, 'Yes, Fulk,' and blundered away, going to and fro through the knee-deep snow, organising the little group of boys, making sure that they understood that they were to use the rope as a guide and never let go. She had them lined up and ready to start when Fulk loomed up beside her. 'Could you manage to bring back a couple of splints—luckily Mr Wallace put a couple in the bus. MacDow has a fractured tib and fib.'

She nodded and urged the boys to get started. It wasn't far, but the snow was deep and the rope awkward to hold, but they made it at last and she opened the bus door in almost tearful relief and helped the boys on board. They were cold and frightened too and she would have liked to have given them the hot tea, but she must get the splints to Fulk first; she set them rubbing their arms and legs and taking off wet boots, dragged out the splints, and as an afterthought, the folded stretcher she found beside them, and made her unwieldy way back to where Fulk was waiting.

He hailed her with a 'Splendid girl!' when he saw the stretcher, and proceeded to splint the broken leg, using Mr MacDow's scarf as well as his own to tie it on, and when Eleanor would have helped get the schoolmaster on to the stretcher, he waved her on one side, lifting the man gently himself. When he was ready he shouted: 'I hate to ask you, but can you manage the foot end? He's a small man, thank the Lord; I'll have to wind the rope as we go—do you think you can do it?'

She nodded sturdily and they set off slowly because of winding the rope, which somehow he managed to do without putting the stretcher down, a mercy, actually, for she was quite sure that if she had had to put her end down she would never have been able to pick it up again. She was speechless with exhaustion when they arrived at the bus, and when she would have helped Fulk drag the stretcher on board and into the aisle between the boys, he shook his head and told her in a no-nonsense voice to get in first. She scrambled through the door, leaving it open and subsiding on to the nearest seat, feeling peculiar, vaguely aware that two of the boys were hauling on one end of the stretcher, helping Fulk, and that she was going to faint unless she did something about it. But it was Fulk who did that; she felt a great arm steady her while he held a brandy flask to her lips and poured the stuff relentlessly down her throat. She choked, said 'Ugh!' and felt almost at once much better.

'How silly of me,' she declared stoutly, and met his dark concerned gaze firmly. 'I'm fine,' she told him, feeling dreadful. 'I'll get some hot tea into these boys before we start back.'

Just for a moment she thought that he was going to kiss her again, but he only smiled briefly, took the brandy from her and said: 'I'll follow behind with this, but MacDow first, I think, though I daresay he will prefer whisky.'

She managed a smile at that and fetched the tea, doling it out into the plastic beakers her mother had thoughtfully provided. The boys were being very good, even laughing a little as they struggled out of their wet coats and boots. She went up and down the bus, pouring the drinks down their willing throats, handing out biscuits, climbing carefully over poor Mr MacDow, lying on the floor in everyone's way; he was feeling easier now; he had come to nicely and the whisky had put fresh heart into him so that he took the biscuit she offered him and nibbled at it.

The bus seemed quite crowded, what with a dozen small boys, recovering their spirits fast, the stretcher, herself and Fulk; there was a lot of melting snow too, and Eleanor, feeling an icy trickle in her neck, wondered which was worse, to be numb with cold or horribly damp. She forgot the unpleasantness of both these sensations in the sheer fright of the return journey. The boys more or less settled and Mr MacDow as comfortable as he could be made, she took her seat by Fulk once more, sitting speechless while he manoeuvred the bus backwards on to the road again, an undertaking which took some considerable time, and on their way at length, staring out at the white waste around her through the curtain of snow, she felt a strong urge to beg him not to go another inch, to stop just where he was and let someone come and rescue them; an absurd idea, bred from cowardice, she chided herself silently, and closed her eyes to shut out the awful possibilities waiting in store for them on the way down. She opened them almost immediately; if he could sit there driving so calmly, then she could at least do her part. 'You need to keep a bit to the left,' she warned him. 'I'll tell you when we reach the corner—shall we have to get out and dig again?'

'Probably, but not you this time—I'll take a couple of the bigger boys with me.'

Which he did, and after that the journey became rather less of a nightmare; true, they skidded and bumped around and once shot across the road in an alarming manner, but the road was easier to make out as they descended it, so that she was able to leave her seat from time to time to see how the boys were faring, wrapping them more closely in blankets and taking round more biscuits. It was a relief to find that Mr MacDow had gone to sleep.

She could hardly believe it when the bus

rocked to an uneasy halt and Fulk shouted: 'Everybody out—one at a time and no shoving!'

Every house in the village had its lights on and the school house doors were standing wide; willing helpers helped the children out of the bus and hustled them inside where anxious mothers claimed their offspring and began the task of getting them into dry clothes, feeding them hot milk and massaging cold arms and legs. There were no men back yet, Mr Wallace told them, but he had done them proud, with a roaring stove and hot drinks and offers of help to get the children to their homes. They lifted Mr MacDow out last of all and carried him to the warmth of the stove and Eleanor, getting awkwardly out of her anorak and kicking off her boots, paused only long enough to call a brief 'Hullo,' to her father before going to help Fulk. The leg was set as well as it could be done with what they had at their disposal, and Mr MacDow, very white, was given another generous dose of whisky before Fulk asked: 'Is there a telephone working?'

Mr MacFarlane shook his head. 'I'm afraid not. The most I can promise is that the moment it's possible they'll get it mended—they're very quick about it. Should MacDow be in hospital?'

'It would be better for him, though it's possible to manage as we are. Shall I just take a quick look at the boys? Those who live near enough could go home, the rest will have to be given a bed for the night. I've my case in the car, I'll give MacDow something to ease the pain and get him home too. Is there someone to look after him?'

'His wife—she's expecting a baby, though.' Eleanor sounded doubtful.

'In that case, if she would be so kind as to put me up for the night I could keep an eye on him.' He glanced round. 'If I could have a hand, we could get him home—but we had better check the boys first.'

A job which was quickly done. The boys seemed little the worse for their adventure, in fact, now that it was all over, they were beginning to enjoy themselves. They went, one by one, escorted by mothers, grannies and big sisters, until there was only Henry left.

Fulk collected Mr Wallace and old Mr MacNab, who had stayed to help with the schoolmaster. 'We'll go now. Eleanor, stay here with your father and Henry, I'll be back in ten minutes.'

'Why?' She was a little impatient; she wanted to get home and eat a huge meal and then go to bed and sleep the clock round.

He didn't answer her directly, only said: 'Ten minutes,' and went away, leaving the three of them by the stove. Eleanor fell asleep at once and only roused when Fulk's voice wakened her with: 'Come on, home.'

She looked at him owl-eyed, said 'Oh,' in a lost voice and got herself to her feet, dragging on her anorak and boots once more and hunting for her torch, and then following the others out into the cold night. The snow had slowed its mad pace and the wind, although strong, was no longer a gale. It was dark too, for the electricity had failed while she slept. It was a miracle that it had survived so long, but they had their torches and with Fulk leading the way, battled their way in single file until the dim light from the oil lamp in the manse hall told them that they were home.

Mrs MacFarlane had the door open before they could reach it, and whatever worry she had felt she effectively concealed now. 'Into the sitting room,' she greeted them. 'There's hot coffee ready and while you're drinking it I'll get Henry into a hot bath——he can have his supper in bed.' She smiled at them all, although her eyes anxiously sought Fulk's face. 'He's all right, Fulk?'

He smiled reassuringly. 'Cold and hungry, that's all. Bed and bath are just the thing. He behaved splendidly——they all did.'

Henry puffed out his chest. 'I wasn't really frightened,' he declared, 'though it was very cold.'

His mother put a hand on his shoulder. 'You shall tell me all about it, dear, but we mustn't be too long; Eleanor will want a bath too—and Fulk.' She glanced round as they were leaving the room. 'You'll spend the night, Fulk?'

He explained about spending the night at Mr MacDow's house. 'But I would love a bath, if I may. . .'

Mrs MacFarlane nodded briskly. 'Of course, and you'll stay for supper too—they won't expect you back for a little while, will they? I'm on edge to hear all about it, but first things first.' With which words she led Henry upstairs.

They had their supper round the fire. Eleanor, warm at last from her bath, her hair plaited tidily and wrapped in a thick dressing gown, could have slept sitting there. She spooned her soup slowly, content to be back home and safe with Fulk sitting unconcernedly opposite her. She frowned a little, her tired mind grappling with the fact that it was possible to like someone very much even when one didn't like him at all. It didn't make sense, and she gave up presently, thinking that it was absurd to suppose that she had ever not liked him. After all, she had been a very little girl when she had vowed to hate him for ever—and a girl had a right to change her mind. She smiled sleepily at him and was strangely disturbed at his intent, unsmiling look. He said good night very shortly afterwards, and Eleanor went upstairs to bed, to wake in the night and wonder about that look. She turned over and curled herself into a ball under the bedclothes; probably they would bicker just as they always did when next they met. It would be nice if they didn't, she thought sleepily as she closed her eyes again.

CHAPTER FOUR

THE bright sunshine and complete lack of
wind just didn't seem true the next morning.
Eleanor took an astonished look out of the
window, dressed quickly in an elderly kilt
and thick jersey, and went downstairs to
breakfast. Her mother looked up as she went
into the kitchen. 'There you are, darling,' she
said happily. 'How lovely to have yesterday
over and done with. Breakfast's ready—
don't forget it's church at ten o'clock.'

Eleanor nodded. 'I hadn't forgotten,
Mother, but there'll be time to clear the path
before I need to dress.' She carried the plates
to the table and went to call Henry. 'When's
Margaret coming back?' she asked as they
sat down at the table.

'As soon as the snow plough clears the
road, and I imagine they will be out
already—that was a freak blizzard, it didn't
get far. The men were telling me that the
telephone was still working between Durness
and the west coast, although the lines were
down to the south of us, and beyond Lairg
the roads are pretty clear. I wonder how Fulk

got on at the MacDows'.' He glanced at his son. 'Henry, are you not hungry?'

Three pairs of eyes stared at the youngest member of the family. Usually he ate as much as the three of them together, but now, this morning he was pecking at his food in a manner totally unlike him.

'Do you feel ill, darling?' his mother asked anxiously.

'I'm just not hungry——I expect I'll eat an enormous dinner to make up for it.'

Eleanor studied him unobtrusively; he looked all right, a little pale perhaps, and certainly listless; could be that he hadn't got over his chickenpox as well as they thought he had. Doctor MacClew might go over him again——she hoped worriedly that the boy hadn't caught a chill; it would be a miracle if they all escaped with nothing at all.

She had intended asking Henry to help her with the snow on the path between the manse and the little church, but instead she helped her mother wash up, made the beds and went outside on her own. There was still an hour before church and the exercise would do her good. She was almost ready when a large hand came down on hers, so that she was forced to stop shovelling.

'Good morning,' said Fulk. 'None the worse for our little adventure, I see. Here, give me that and go and make yourself decent for church.'

'No, I won't,' said Eleanor immediately. 'For one thing, I'm dressed for it and you're not.'

He still had her hand fast. 'And for the other thing?' he prompted her softly.

'Well, I don't much like being told what to do.' She looked up at him and the question tripped off her tongue before she could stop it. 'Does Imogen do exactly as you say?'

He didn't look in the least put out, only a little surprised. 'It's hard to say; I don't remember any occasion when it was necessary for me to ask her to do anything.'

She blinked. 'How funny!'

The dark eyes became cold, he said silkily: 'Funny? Perhaps you would explain. . .'

She said hastily: 'I didn't mean funny funny—just strange. Don't you see much of each other?' She went on staring at him, asking for trouble and not much caring.

'I hardly feel that it is any of your business, Eleanor, and if you're trying to cast doubts into my head, I can assure you that it's a waste of time.' His voice was as cold as his eyes; he wasn't bothering to conceal his anger. But she was angry too now, with him and with herself for starting the whole miserable conversation in the first place.

'You're awful,' she said, making it even worse, 'just as bad as you used to be; I might have known. . .I thought just once or twice that I'd been mistaken, that you'd changed, but you haven't.' She tossed her head. 'Here, take the beastly shovel!' Her glance swept over his undoubtedly expensive tweeds and well-tailored camel hair topcoat. 'You'll look very silly shovelling snow in Savile Row suiting, but that's your affair!'

She flounced back indoors, muttering at his roar of laughter.

When she came downstairs twenty minutes later, in her tweed coat and little fur hat, it was to find him in the sitting room, talking to the rest of the family, and he looked as though he had never seen a snow shovel in his life. He got to his feet as she went in and said gravely: 'I like that hat,' and added to the room at large: 'It's surprising what clothes do for a woman.'

Her father turned round to look at her. 'Indeed, yes. Fulk is quite right, my dear, that is a pretty hat, though I thought you looked very nice yesterday in that hooded thing.'

'Father, my oldest anorak!'

'Your father's got something there—you did look nice. You looked sensible and trust-worthy too, exactly the kind of companion a man wants when he's on a ticklish job.'

She gasped. 'Well, I never. . .after all the things you said!'

He grinned. 'Coals of fire, Eleanor.'

'A whole scuttle of them—what's come over you?'

He answered lightly, 'Oh, a change of heart,' and got to his feet again. 'Ought we to be on our way?'

The church was very full. Even those who usually attended only upon special occasions had turned up, deeming yesterday's occurrence well worth a few prayers of thanks. The small building, bursting at the seams, rocked to the thankful voices, and Eleanor, who sang quite well in an amateurish way, sang too, a little off-key on the top notes but making up for that by her enthusiasm. Fulk, standing beside her, glanced at her several times, and Mrs MacFarlane, watching him, wondered if her daughter's slightly off-key rendering of the hymns nettled him at all, then changed her mind when she saw the little smile tugging the corners of his mouth.

Fulk went back to the MacDows' house after church, casually taking Eleanor with him. 'And before you fly into a temper because you don't want to come,' he informed her as soon as they were out of earshot of the rest of the family, 'I want to ask you something. Does Henry strike you as being his usual self?'

'Oh, you've noticed it, too,' she exclaimed, quite forgetting that she had intended to be coolly polite and nothing more. 'You don't think he's sickening for something?'

'I can't tell, but I had an idea in church. Would your mother and father allow him to come and stay with me for a few weeks?' He saw her sudden look of alarm. 'No, don't instantly suspect that he's dying of some obscure disease—he's a tough little boy and healthy enough, but he has a good brain, much above average, I should imagine, and he tends to work it too hard. A holiday wouldn't do him any harm, away from lessons and even the remote chance of going to school. I'll keep a fatherly eye on him and he'll be free to roam where he likes. I live in the country, you know, and there's plenty for him to do. I'll see that if he must read, it will be nothing to tease that brain of his. . .'

They were almost at the MacDow croft. 'Why are you doing it?' asked Eleanor, then wished she hadn't spoken, for it sounded rude and for the moment at any rate, they were friends. But Fulk only answered placidly: 'I like the boy.'

'It's a marvellous idea,' she ruminated,

half aloud, and then choosing her words carefully: 'Will there be anyone else? I mean, does anyone else live in your house?'

His smile held a tinge of mockery. 'Still determined to think the worst of me, Eleanor?' And when she said sharply: 'No, of course not,' he went on smoothly: 'I've a housekeeper, a good sort who will feed Henry like a fighting cock—there are a couple of other people around too, but Imogen won't be there; that's what you really wanted to know, wasn't it? And if you credit me with entertaining young women while she's away then I must disappoint you—my household would do credit to a monk.'

'I can't think why you should suppose me to be interested in your private life,' declared Eleanor haughtily. She tossed her head rather grandly, tripped up on a hidden lump of snow and fell flat on her face. Fulk scooped her up, stood her on her feet, brushed her down, kissed her swiftly and said gently: 'There's no need to get uppity.' A remark she didn't have time to answer because they were on the doorstep and Mrs MacDow was opening the door.

The schoolmaster was sitting in a chair drawn up to the fire, a pair of very out-of-date crutches by his side. He greeted them cheerfully and when Eleanor expressed surprise at seeing him there in his dressing gown, smoking his pipe and looking almost normal, he laughed and assured her that it was all the doctor's doing.

'Not ideal,' murmured Fulk. 'The crutches are heirlooms from some bygone age, but they'll do until we can get you into Durness. They'll do an X-ray and put the leg in plaster and a walking iron—all you'll need then is a good stout stick.'

They stayed talking for a few minutes, lighthearted argument as to the ill-fated climbing expedition. 'We should have been in a pretty bad way if you hadn't come along,' said Mr MacDow. 'We knew a search party would come out after us sooner or later, but if they'd waited until there were enough men, the boys would have been in poor shape to tackle the scramble down. That was a brilliant idea bringing the bus, though how you managed to get it up there beats me.'

'We had our difficult moments,' Fulk acknowledged. 'Luckily Eleanor proved to be a sort of pocket compass.'

They looked at her and she went a faint pink, so that she looked quite eye-catching, what with flushed cheeks and the fur hat crowning her brown hair. 'I couldn't have driven the bus,' she pointed out, 'and if the men had been here they would have found the way just as well—better, perhaps.'

'They wouldn't have fancied taking that bus,' declared the schoolmaster. 'We'll be indebted to you, Doctor—I doubt if we'll ever be able to do the same for you, but you've made a great many friends in the village.'

'Thank you—and that reminds me, I wanted a word with you about young Henry. I've spoken to Eleanor already, but I should appreciate your advice before I say anything to Mr MacFarlane.'

Eleanor had to admit that he put his case very well; Mr MacDow agreed whole-heartedly that Henry was far too clever for his age. 'A real boy, make no mistake about that,' he observed, 'but the laddie tires himself out, reading beyond his years; working away at problems, wanting to know this, that and the other. He could miss a few weeks at school and never know the difference. If you say it would do the boy some good then I'll not say nay, Doctor, provided his father hasn't any objection.'

The pastor had no objection at all and his wife was openly delighted. 'What a dear man you are, Fulk,' she exclaimed. 'It's just what will do him the most good; his head is stuffed with algebra and science and learning to play chess, and there's no stopping him.' She looked so happy and relieved that Eleanor bent to kiss her swiftly in understanding. 'He's over in the loft,' said Mrs MacFarlane, 'feeding Mrs Trot and the kittens, do go and tell him yourself.' She added in an offhand way, 'Go with Fulk, will you, Eleanor? Henry forgot to take the milk with him, and Mrs Trot will need it before the evening.'

Henry was sitting where his big sister usually sat, on the floor with the kittens playing round him, while Mrs Trot ate her dinner. He had heard them on the ladder and turned his head to watch them. 'I thought it was you,' he remarked. 'It isn't our dinnertime yet, is it?'

'Almost.' Eleanor chose an apple and offered it to Fulk before taking one for herself; they shared the sack of potatoes and munched contentedly for a minute or two until Fulk asked: 'Henry, how do you feel about spending a week or two with me in Holland?'

The little boy's face became one large grin. 'Me? Honour bright? Just me? Oh, Fulk, how absolutely smashing!' The grin faded. 'I have to have a passport. I was reading about that the other day—I haven't got one.'

'That's OK, that can be arranged, but we'll need to go to Glasgow for it. I tell you what, if I take Eleanor back tomorrow, you could come with us and we could see about it on the way—that's provided the roads are clear. We can get your photo taken and go to the Passport Office and see what they can do for us. If it's OK, we'll come back here and pack your bags.'

'Oh, golly!' Henry was on his feet, capering round the bare boards, only to stop abruptly. 'I'll have to leave the kittens.' His face fell as he picked up the smallest and ugliest of them, the one no one wanted. 'No one's offered for Moggy.'

Eleanor felt a glow of warmth as Fulk exclaimed instantly: 'I will—I've a dog and my housekeeper has a cat of her own, but we could do with a kitten. We'll take him with us.'

'I say—really? You mean that, Fulk?'

'I mean it—I'm partial to kittens around the house.'

Eleanor's tongue was too quick for her once more. 'Supposing your Imogen doesn't like him?'

Fulk turned a bland face to hers. 'My dear girl, don't you know that people in love are prepared to do anything for the loved one's sake?'

An observation which depressed her very much; quite possibly Imogen was a very nice girl, prepared to sacrifice her own likes and dislikes just to please Fulk; which was a pity, because it was hard to dislike a nice girl, and she had made up her mind to dislike Imogen. She contented herself by saying: 'Well, I wouldn't know about that. I say, there's really no need to take me back tomorrow—Edinburgh will be right out of your way, and the roads. . .'

'Nervous? Surely not after yesterday's little trip. We can go via Glasgow and if there's any hitch or waiting about to be done, we can take you to the hospital and then go back there.'

He made it all sound so easy—convenient, almost. She found herself agreeing with him as Henry tidied the kittens back into their box, planted Mrs Trot beside them and announced that he was quite ready for his dinner.

The meal was an animated one, with everyone talking at once, and Eleanor was the only one, so she thought, to notice that Henry ate hardly anything at all. But she wasn't; she looked up and caught Fulk's eyes upon her and knew that he had seen it too and wasn't going to say anything. Obedient to that dark glance, she didn't say anything either.

The snow ploughs and the weather had done their work by morning; the roads were clear, the telephone and the electricity were once more functioning and although there was a good deal of snow still lying around it wasn't likely to hinder them much. Fulk was at the manse by half past ten, having got up early and driven Mr MacDow, wedged on to the back seat, into Durness, where they had X-rayed the limb, clapped it in plaster and a walking iron and handed him back to Fulk, who had in turn handed him over to his own doctor's care. He brought the news that the road to Lairg was more or less clear and beyond that there should be no difficulties, and they left at once, stopping to lunch in Inverness at the Station Hotel, where even the magnificence of the restaurant and the remarkable choice of food did little to increase Henry's appetite. Of course, he was excited, thought Eleanor worriedly as she joined in the cheerful talk of her companions. Whatever was wrong with the boy's appetite hadn't affected his spirits.

The Panther made light work of the hundred and seventy miles remaining of their journey, so that they reached the Passport Office with half an hour to spare before it closed for the day and they would have been there sooner, only they had stopped on the way for some instant passport photos of Henry. Eleanor stayed in the little outer office while Fulk and Henry went to see what could be done. It was a dull little room, with nothing to read but pamphlets about emigrating and a stern warning of the dire punishment awaiting anyone who tampered with their passport. She read these interesting titbits of information several times, and then for lack of anything else to do, found paper and pen in her handbag and amused herself making a list of things she would like to buy; it was a long list and imaginative and she headed it boldly 'Things I would like to have,' and underlined it twice. She was on the point of crossing out the more frivolous items when Fulk and Henry came back, looking pleased with themselves; obviously they had been successful. She stood up, dropped her handbag, her gloves and the paper and asked: 'Is it OK?' to the two bent forms scrabbling round on the floor picking up her possessions.

Henry lifted his head. 'Rather. Fulk talked—they were super. We're to call and fetch it when we go.'

'And when's that?'

'The day after tomorrow.' Fulk spoke absentmindedly, Eleanor's piece of paper in one hand. 'What's this—don't tell me I shouldn't read it for it's not a letter. Besides, you shouldn't drop things all over the place so carelessly.'

'I was surprised,' she excused herself. 'It's only a list.'

She put out a hand which he instantly took hold of and held. 'Sable coat,' he read in an interested voice, 'Gina Fratini dress, Givenchy scarf, Marks and Spencer sweater, toothpaste,' he chuckled and went on slowly, 'surgical scissors, every paperback I want, roses for Christmas. Seems a pretty sensible list to me, but why roses for Christmas, Eleanor?'

She tugged at her hand to no good purpose. 'Oh, it's just something silly, you know. . .I mean, if anyone bothered to give me roses, masses of them, I mean, not just six in cellophane—when everyone else was having potted hyacinths and chrysanthemums, I'd know that I meant something to—to someone. . .' She paused because he was looking at her rather strangely. 'Like the sables,' she went on chattily, 'and the Givenchy scarf. . .'

'But not the toothpaste,' he suggested, half laughing.

'No.' She took the odds and ends Henry was holding out to her and stuffed them away and said brightly: 'How nice that everything went off without a hitch. Aren't you wildly excited, Henry?'

Henry said that yes, he was, and began to explain exactly how a passport was issued and the conditions imposed. 'And wasn't it clever of Fulk to know that he had to have a letter from Father to show them?' he demanded. 'I shall be glad when I'm grown up and can do those sort of things.' He cast a disparaging look at his surroundings. 'May we go soon?'

Fulk took them to tea; to the Central Hotel, large and impressive with its draperies and its mirrors and chandeliers. Henry looked round, his eyes wide. He had never been in such a place before for his tea, and it was an experience which he was enjoying. Eleanor blessed Fulk for his understanding of a small boy's idea of a treat, and tried not to worry at the small meal her brother was making.

They took her back to Edinburgh when they had finished, going with her to the Nurses' Home door, after a protracted walk across the forecourt because Henry wanted to know exactly where everything was and how many people worked in the hospital for how many hours and how much money. 'I shall be a famous doctor,' he told them, 'a physician, like Fulk. Perhaps I might be your partner—you'll probably be needing one by the time I'm grown up, Fulk.'

'Very probably,' Fulk agreed gravely. 'Now let us say goodbye to Eleanor and make for home, shall we? It's a long drive; you can sit in the back and go to sleep, if you wish.'

'Go to sleep? Of course I shall sit with you in front and watch the dashboard and you can explain. . .'

'You're sure you want him?' asked Eleanor, giving her brother a hug and looking anxiously at Fulk over his small shoulder.

'Quite sure.' He smiled and held out his hand. 'Don't work too hard,' he advised her, and didn't say goodbye, only put her case inside the door for her and then cast an arm round Henry's bony frame and turned away. She was tempted to delay them with some question or other; she didn't want to be left, but she remembered that he had a journey of many hours before him. She went through the door and closed it quietly without looking back.

She felt bad-tempered in the morning, due, she told herself, to the long car journey the day before and all the excitement during the blizzard. That it might also be due to the fact that Fulk hadn't bothered to say goodbye to her was something she had no intention of admitting, not even to herself. Despite her best efforts, she was snappy with the nurses and found the patients tiresome too, and making the excuse that she had to wash her hair and make a telephone call home, she didn't go, as she usually did, to the Sisters' sitting room when she got off duty, but retired to her room, where she sat on her bed and brooded.

Hunger drove her down to supper, and in the babble of talk round the table, her unusual quietness was hardly noticed, although several of her closer friends wondered if she were starting a cold or merely feeling unsettled after her weekend. Probably the latter, they decided, and bore her off to drink tea with them, carefully not asking questions. Someone had asked her at breakfast that morning if she had found the blizzard very awful and she had answered so briefly that they had concluded that for some reason or other she didn't want to talk about it.

She felt a little better the next morning, though; she was a girl with plenty of common sense, to let herself be put out by something which wasn't important to her was plain foolish; she went on duty determined to be nice to everyone and succeeded very well, plunging into the daily problems of the ward with zest, listening to Miss Tremble's everlasting grumbles and conducting a round with Sir Arthur and his retinue with her usual good humour and efficiency. It was at the end of this time-consuming exercise that he, sipping coffee in her office, remarked: 'You look washed out, Sister. Shovelling snow evidently doesn't agree with you.'

'Shovel...how did you know that, sir?' She put down her cup and eyed him in some surprise.

'Van Hensum told me—he must have worked you too hard.'

She rushed to Fulk's defence. 'No—indeed no, Sir Arthur, I did very little, he was the one who did everything.'

'H'm, well—he didn't mention his own activities.'

She told her companion at some length, sparing no details. 'So you see,' she concluded, 'he was pretty super.' She frowned; the whole family had got into the habit of using Henry's favourite word. 'He...' she began; there was no other word—'He was super.'

Sir Arthur studied his nails and hid a smile. 'I have always found Doctor van Hensum—er—pretty super myself, purely from a professional point of view, of course.' He got up. 'Many thanks for the coffee, Sister.' He glanced at his watch. 'Dear me, is that the time?' He wandered to the door and she accompanied him down the short corridor which led to the swing doors, where he nodded affably, muttered something about being late as usual and hurried away.

Eleanor went back into the ward and plunged into her work once more. The temptation to sit down somewhere quiet and think about Fulk was tempting but pointless. Her mind edged away from the idea that it would be nice if he were to call with Henry on their way to Holland, but Fulk didn't do things to oblige people, only to please himself. This glaring untruth caused her to frown so heavily that Bob Wise, the Medical Officer on duty, walking down the ward to meet her, asked: 'I say, are you angry with me about something?'

She hastened to deny it with such friendliness that he was emboldened to ask her to go out with him that evening. A film, he suggested diffidently, and brightened visibly when she agreed. He was a pleasant young man, very English; he had paid her what she realized was a rare compliment when he had first come to the hospital, telling her that she spoke like an English girl, a remark which she rightly guessed had been born from homesickness and the girl he had left behind him. They had become casual friends since then and from time to time spent an evening together.

So she went to the cinema with him and afterwards sat over a cup of coffee with him in a nearby café, while he told her the latest news of his Maureen. They had known each other since childhood; he had told her that the first time they had met, and their plans had been settled long ago. Eleanor, listening to him discussing the wedding which was at least two years away, wondered what it would be like to have your future cut and dried; to know that you would never be tempted to fall in love with anyone else—it would be wonderful to be as sure as that. She had fancied herself in love on several occasions, of course, but never so deeply that she had felt that life would stop for her when she fell out of it again. Her mother had declared on more than one occasion that she was hard to please; perhaps she was. She sighed a little and begged Bob to describe, just once more, the engagement ring he had bestowed upon Maureen.

She was so busy the next morning that she had no time to think of anything at all but her work. She heaved a sigh when she had dished the dinners, sent most of the nurses to their own meal, and started on her second round of the day, this time accompanied by the most junior nurse on her staff. They tidied beds as they went, made the patients comfortable for their short afternoon nap, and under Eleanor's experienced eye the little nurse took temperatures, had a go at the blood pressures, and charted the diabetics. They had reached Miss Tremble's bed and were, as usual, arguing with that lady, this time about the freshness of the lettuce she had had on her dinner plate, when she broke off her diatribe to say: 'Here's that nice doctor again, Sister.'

Eleanor managed not to turn round and take a look, but the little nurse did. 'Ooh, isn't he groovy—I think he's in a hurry, Sister.'

She couldn't go on pretending that he wasn't there. She turned round and started to walk down the ward towards him with Miss Tremble's urgent: 'And don't forget that we haven't finished our discussion, Sister,' and the little nurse, uncertain as to what she should do, dogging her footsteps.

Fulk was businesslike. 'Forgive me for coming into the ward without asking you first, Sister,' he said, all politeness. 'I did mention it to Sir Arthur, but it seemed best not to telephone you.' He smiled: 'We are rather short of time.'

'We?'

'Henry is here too and dying to see you. I hope you won't mind, I left him in your office.' He glanced at the little nurse and gave her a nice smile. 'Could Nurse keep an eye on the ward for a couple of minutes while you say goodbye to him?'

'Yes, of course. Nurse Angus, you could take Miss Robertson's temp, and have a go at her BP too—I'll only be a moment.'

She walked down the ward beside Fulk without speaking, partly because he was behaving like a consultant again and partly because she couldn't think of anything to say, but once through the door and in the office with Henry prancing round her, Fulk became Fulk once more, his dark face alight with amusement. 'Well, Henry,' he asked, 'I'm right, aren't I? She doesn't look like Eleanor at all, does she?'

She stood while they looked her over slowly. 'No,' said her brother at last, 'she doesn't. I like you better with your hair hanging down your back, Eleanor, and up an apple tree or fishing, though you look very important in that funny cap.' He looked at Fulk. 'Don't you like her better when she's home?' he appealed.

'Oh, rather. She terrifies me like this, all no-nonsense and starch.' Fulk grinned at her. 'Looking at you now,' he declared thoughtfully, 'I can see that you have changed quite a bit since you were five—for the better. I am not of course discussing your character.'

He gave her no time to answer this, but: 'We have to go, we're on our way to Hull. Henry wants to know when he can telephone you once we get home.'

'I'm off until one o'clock tomorrow—will you have got there by then?'

'Lord, yes. Say goodbye, boy, or we shall miss the ferry.'

She bent to Henry's hug, slipped some money into his hand and begged him to send her a postcard or two, then gave him a sisterly pat on the back, for Fulk was already at the door. 'Have fun,' she said, and added a casual goodbye to Fulk who, although he had said nothing, she felt sure was impatient to be gone, but he came back from the door.

'Don't I get a kiss too?' he asked at his silkiest, and not waiting for her to speak her mind, bent his head.

When they had gone she stood looking at the closed door; Henry had kissed her with childish enthusiasm, but Fulk's technique had been perfect; moreover the enthusiasm hadn't been lacking, either.

INGER FOR CHRISTMAS   99

He gave her no time to answer this, but
'We have to say, we have our way to Hull,
Henry wants to know when he can telephone
you once we get home.'
'I'm off now—tomorrow—tomorrow I will
you have got there by then.'

CHAPTER FIVE

HENRY telephoned the next day, his breathless voice gabbling excitedly over the wire
into her interested ear. The journey had been
super, so had the Panther, so was Fulk's
house, and Moggy hadn't minded the dog at
all and had settled down very well and wasn't
that super too?

Eleanor agreed that everything was just as
super as it could be; she wasn't going to get
any interesting details from him, that was
apparent, and she was disappointed when he
rang off without any mention of Fulk other
than a highly detailed account of his driving.

A series of postcards followed, inscribed
in her brother's childish hand, and from the
sparse information they conveyed, she concluded that life for him was just about as
perfect as a small boy could wish for,
although exactly what made it so wasn't
clear, and when she telephoned her mother
it was to hear that his letters home were
almost as brief as the cards he sent and exas-
peratingly devoid of detail.

It was almost a week after Henry had gone

that he mentioned, on a particularly colourful postcard, that his throat was a bit sore; the information had been sandwiched between the statement that he had been to a museum at Leeuwarden, and had eaten something called *poffertjes* for his supper, so that she had scarcely noted it. Mrs MacFarlane had written to say that Fulk had telephoned several times to say that Henry appeared to be enjoying himself, so much so that on the last occasion he had suggested that the boy might like to spend another week or so with him so that he could be in Holland for the feast of Sint Nikolaas. 'And of course your father and I said yes at once,' wrote her mother. 'How kind Fulk is.'

Very kind, Eleanor had to agree, feeling somehow deflated as she finished the letter and hurried off to change out of uniform. Perry Maddon, the Casualty Officer, was taking her to the theatre that evening and she was quite looking forward to it; he was another nice lad, she thought as she slid swiftly into a plain wool dress, but she would have to take care not to encourage him. At the moment they were good friends and that, as far as she was concerned, was how it was going to stay. He wasn't the man she could marry—she didn't give herself time to consider the matter further, but caught up her coat and made for the hospital entrance.

The evening was a success, the play had been amusing and afterwards they had coffee and sandwiches at the Blue Bird and walked down the road to the hospital, talking lightly about nothing in particular. It had been a pleasant evening, Eleanor decided as she tumbled into bed, so why had she this sudden feeling of impending disaster? So strong that it was keeping her awake. It couldn't be the ward; Miss Tremble, usually the root of any trouble, had been perfectly all right all day, and although there were several ill patients she didn't think that they would take a dramatic turn for the worse. She did a mental round of the ward in her sleepy head, trying to pinpoint the probable cause of her disquiet. 'My silly fancy,' she chided herself out loud, and went at last to sleep.

Only it wasn't fancy; Fulk van Hensum came the next day, walking into the ward as she served the patients' dinners from the heated trolley in the middle of the ward. She was facing away from the door so she didn't see him come in, but the little nurse, her hand outstretched to take the plate of steamed fish Eleanor was handing her, said happily: 'He's here again, Sister.'

'And who is here?' queried Eleanor, busy with the next plate. 'Sir Arthur? One of the porters? The Provost himself?'

The little nurse giggled. 'It's that great big man who came last time, Sister.' She smiled widely over Eleanor's shoulder, and Eleanor put down the plate and turned her head to have a look.

It was Fulk all right, standing very still just inside the ward door. He said at once: 'Good day to you all. Sister, might I have a word with you?'

His voice was calm, as was his face, but she went to him at once. 'Something's wrong,' she said, low-voiced. 'Will you tell me, please?' She lifted her lovely eyes to meet his dark steady gaze.

'It's Henry, isn't it?' she added, and took comfort from his reassuring little smile. When he spoke his voice held the considered, measured tones of a doctor and he took her hands in his and held them fast; their grip was very comforting. 'Yes, it's Henry. He has rheumatic fever.'

Her mouth felt dry. 'I remember now, he had a sore throat—he wrote that on one of those postcards. . . Is he—is he very ill?'

'You mean, is he going to die, don't you, my dear? No, he's not. He's very ill but not, I think, dangerously so.' His smile became very gentle. 'If that had been the case I shouldn't have left him, you know.'

'No, of course not. How silly of me, I'm sorry. Is he in hospital?'

Fulk's brows rose a little. 'Certainly not. He's at my home with two excellent nurses to look after him. The only thing is, he wants you, Eleanor.'

'Then I must go to him——may I come back with you?' She raced on, thinking out loud without giving him a chance to answer her. 'No, that won't do——I expect you're over here on business of your own, but I could go tonight. They probably won't give me leave, but I shall go just the same. I must telephone Mother first, though, and you'll have to tell me where you live——you wouldn't mind, would you?'

He had her hands still in his. 'Dear girl, how you do run on, and there's no need. I'm here to take you to Henry; I've already telephoned your parents and I've been to see your Principal Nursing Officer. You're free to go just as soon as you can hand over to your staff nurse. I'm on my way to Tongue now to fetch Margaret; she's coming too, for when Henry feels better he'll want to be up and about, and he mustn't do too much too soon, you know that as well as I——I thought she might help to amuse him during his enforced idleness. She will be ready and waiting for me; we'll be back to pick you up within a few hours.'

She looked at him in bewilderment. 'Fulk, Tongue's three hundred miles from here, even in that car of yours it would take you hours. . .'

'Of course it would, but I've a plane to fly me up to Wick, and as good luck would have it, James is at the manse and will drive Margaret to the airport to meet me; we should both arrive there at about the same time and be back here without much time lost.'

She smiled rather shakily at him. 'You've thought of everything. Thank you, Fulk. Tell me what time I'm to be ready and where I'm to meet you.'

'Good girl!' He looked at his watch. 'There'll be a taxi to take you to the airport— can you be ready by five o'clock? You may have to wait for a little while, for I'm not sure just how long we shall be. Bring enough luggage for a couple of weeks—and don't forget your passport, and when you get to the airport go to the booking hall and wait until we come. OK?'

Eleanor nodded. 'Yes. Oh, Fulk, how kind you are—I feel so mean. . .'

He didn't ask her why she felt mean, only smiled faintly and gave her back her hands.

'Go and finish those dinners,' he advised her. '*Tot ziens.*'

A little over four hours later, sitting quietly in the airport, her one piece of luggage at her feet, Eleanor had the leisure to look back over the afternoon. It had been all rush and bustle, of course, but there had been no difficulties; Fulk must have seen to those. She had merely done exactly as he had told her to do, trying not to think too much about Henry, keeping her mind on prosaic things, like what to wear and what to pack. She had taken the minimum of everything in the end, and worn her warm tweed coat over a green jersey dress, and because it was a cold evening and it might be even colder in Holland, she had put on the little fur hat and the fur-lined gloves she had bought herself only that week. She looked very nice, and several men turned to give her a second look, although she was quite unaware of this— indeed, she was unaware of Fulk standing a little way off, looking at her too, until she had a feeling that she was being watched, and when she saw who it was she stood up quickly, relief sending a faint colour into her pale face as he walked over to her and picked up her baggage.

'You haven't been waiting too long?' he

asked. 'Margaret's waiting in the plane—if you're ready?'

Perhaps he was tired, she thought as she walked beside him; his voice had sounded austere and formal, as though her being there annoyed him. Perhaps it did, but it was no time to split hairs as to who liked whom or didn't. Henry was the only one who mattered. She followed him through the formalities, taken aback to find that he had chartered a plane to take them over to Holland; she had supposed that they were going on a normal flight, but perhaps there wasn't a direct flight to Groningen. It must be costing him the earth, she worried silently, but there wasn't time to think about that now; Margaret, waiting eagerly for them, was full of messages from her mother and father and questions about Henry, all jumbled up with excited talk about her journey. 'And wasn't it lucky that I had my passport for that school trip last summer,' she wanted to know, 'and that James was home. There's a letter from Mother in my pocket. She's very worried, but she says she knows Henry's going to be all right with you and Fulk there—Oh, look, we're moving!'

It was only when they were airborne and Margaret had become silent enough for Eleanor to gather her wits together that she realized what the journey had entailed for Fulk. He had been very efficient and it must have taken his precious time—consultants hadn't all that time to spare from their work—and the cost. . .her mind boggled at that. She turned round to where he was sitting behind them, wanting to tell him how grateful she was, and found him asleep. He looked different now, the faint arrogance which she detected from time to time in his face had gone. He bore the look of a tired man enjoying an untroubled nap, and for some reason it put her in mind of that time, so long ago, when he had picked her up and comforted her. He had been safe then, he was safe now; nothing could happen to her. . . Her face softened and she smiled faintly, then composed her face quickly, but not quickly enough.

'Now, why do you look at me like that?' demanded Fulk softly. 'I could almost delude myself into believing that you had changed your opinion of me.'

'You have been very kind,' she began primly, and he grinned.

'Ah, back to normal and that disapproving tone of yours.'

'That's unfair!' she cried. 'I was just going to thank you for being so absolutely marvellous, and now you mock at me and it's impossible for me to say it. . .'

'So don't, dear girl; my motives have been purely selfish, you know. If you're with Henry I shall feel free to come and go as I please.'

'That's not true—of all the silly tales! You know as well as I do. . .' She stopped and looked away for a moment and then back again at his smiling face. 'I'm truly grateful.'

He said, gently mocking: 'That I should live to see the day when Eleanor MacFarlane is grateful to me,' and then, before she could protest at that: 'What is in that cardboard box?'

'Crowdie—Henry loves it. I thought, when he gets better and begins to eat, he might like it on his bread and butter. There's a little Orkney cheese too. They'll keep in the fridge—you've got one, haven't you?'

There was a gleam at the back of his eyes. 'I believe so—if not, I'll get one the moment we arrive.'

She looked at him in astonishment. 'But surely you must know what you've got in your own house?'

'Well, I'm a busy man, you know—I tend to leave such things to my housekeeper.'

'The sooner you have a wife, the better,' declared Eleanor matter-of-factly. 'She'll see to your household. I expect your housekeeper will be glad to have someone to consult about such things.'

'Well, I shall have a wife soon, shan't I?' His voice was meek. 'Though I have a strong feeling that Imogen won't wish to be bothered with such things as fridges—she isn't very interested in the kitchen.'

'Oh, I'm sure she will be once you're married,' said Eleanor hearteningly.

'And you? Do you like the kitchen, Eleanor?'

She drew Margaret's sleeping head on to her shoulder. 'Yes, of course, but it wouldn't do if I didn't, living where we do—you've seen for yourself how far away it is; we have to be independent of shops, you know.'

'You don't hanker after the bright lights?' He asked the question half seriously.

'No—at least I don't think so; I don't know much about them.'

'So if some man living at the back of beyond wanted to marry you, you wouldn't hesitate to say yes?'

'If I loved him I wouldn't hesitate, but then it wouldn't matter where he lived.'

He gave a little nod, much in the manner of one who had solved himself a problem. 'Is Margaret asleep?' and when she said yes: 'You had better close your own eyes—it may be well past your bedtime by the time you get your sleep tonight.' His voice was cold and formal again, he closed his eyes as he spoke and she looked at him indignantly; he had a nasty way of making her feel, when it suited him, of no account.

Hours later, sitting by Henry's bed, holding his hot hand in hers, she had all the time in the world to concede that Fulk's advice had been good. She had dozed off, still indignant, and had only wakened as they came in to land at Eelde airport, a little to the south of Groningen, where she and Margaret had been bustled out with ruthless efficiency by Fulk, guided through Customs and told to get into the back seat of the waiting Panther, and when Margaret had declared with sleepy peevishness that she was hungry and wanted to go to bed, he had told her with bracing kindness that she would be given her supper in no time at all and be tucked up in bed before she knew where she was; he gave Eleanor no such assurance, though, and she bit back the yawn she longed to give and tried to appear alert and wide awake. Not that that had mattered at all, for he didn't look back at her once, which didn't stop her asking the back of his head: 'Do you live in Groningen? Is the city far from here?'

He answered her over a shoulder as he took the car away from the airport approach roads and turned into a country road which seemed to her to be very dark. His voice was a little impatient. 'Ten kilometres to the north, but we only go through the outskirts. I live another eight kilometres further on.' He turned away again, under the impression, she decided crossly, that he had told her all she needed to know of the geographical details. She sat in silence then, Margaret once more asleep beside her, and looked out of the window—not that she had been able to see much, only the road ahead, spotlighted by the car's powerful headlights, but presently the road had woven itself into the city's edge and she gazed out upon the lighted windows of the houses and stared up at the rooftops. It was a pity that it was such a dark night, for she could see so little, and very soon they had left the streets behind them once more and were back in the country. She tried again, being a dogged girl. 'What is the name of the village you live in?'

'I don't live in a village. The nearest one is called Ezingum.' He had sounded impatient still and she had lapsed into silence once more, straining her eyes to see what was outside the window. She was rewarded by a glimpse of water presently—a river, a canal perhaps, never the sea? She wanted to ask the silent man in front of her, but he would only grunt or at best answer her with that same impatience.

She sighed, much louder than she knew, and had been surprised when Fulk said quietly: 'We're almost home,' and turned the car into a narrow lane—but it wasn't a lane; she had caught a glimpse of towering gateposts on either side of the car. It was a drive, running between grass banks with the wintry outlines of larch trees above them. They rounded a bend and Eleanor saw Fulk's house for the first time. Henry had described it as a nice house and she had conjured up a rather vague picture in her mind of a pleasant villa in the residential part of Groningen, but from the number of lighted windows and the impressive porch before which they were stopping, it wasn't in the least like that. This house, even in the semi-dark, was large and solid—the manse would probably fit very nicely into its hall. She had wakened Margaret then, hushed her fretful voice demanding to know where they were, and got out of the car because Fulk had opened the door for her. As she stood beside him on the smooth gravel sweep, he had said briefly: 'Welcome to Huys Hensum, both of you,' then swept them up the steps to the front door, open now and with a little round dumpling of a woman waiting for them.

'Juffrouw Witsma,' he had introduced her, shaking her hand and saying something to her in his own language, and they had all gone into the house. . .

Eleanor looked at the clock, took Henry's pulse, slipped the thermometer under his thin arm, and checked his breathing. His temperature was up a little since she had taken it last. She charted it and looked anxiously at his small white face. He was sleeping now, but he was restless too, although Fulk had expressed satisfaction at his condition. She settled back into her chair and allowed her thoughts to wander once more.

Her first glimpse of the house had taken her off balance; obviously her previous conception of Fulk as being a successful doctor, comfortably off, but no more than that, would have to be scrapped. His home, even at the first glance, had been revealed as old, magnificent and splendidly furnished. He had led them across the lofty square hall, with its polished floor strewn with rugs, its panelled walls and enormous chandelier hanging from an elaborate ceiling, into what she had supposed to be the sitting room, a room large enough to accommodate ten times their number, but somehow homelike with its enormous armchairs and sofas flanking the hooded fireplace, handsomely framed portraits on the walls and a variety of charming table lamps set on fragile tables. He had invited them to sit down, saying that he would go at once to Henry to see how he did. He was back within a short while, reassuring them at once that the boy was holding his own nicely. 'He wants to see you, Eleanor,' he had told her. 'I haven't told him that Margaret is here, time for that when he feels more himself. Juffrouw Witsma has supper ready for us—I suggest that we have it at once so that Margaret can go to bed.'

She had agreed at once, only begging that she might see Henry first, and he had raised no objection, merely remarking that if she didn't mind, he and Margaret would start their meal. 'And then if you are not back, I'll take Margaret up to her room and see her settled in,' he promised, 'but first I will show you where Henry is.'

The stairs were oak and uncarpeted, with a massive banister, and at their top she followed him across a wide landing and down two steps into a little passage, thickly carpeted. With his hand on one of the three doors in it, he turned to her. 'The day nurse is still here, I shall be taking her back to Groningen in the morning, but I arranged with the hospital that unless I telephoned, there would be no need for the night nurse.' He stared down at her, his eyes half hidden by their lids. 'Your room is next door and communicates with his, and he will be quite safe to leave while he is sleeping, but you will do just as you wish—you have only to ask for anything you require and if you would prefer the night nurse to come, I will see to it at once.'

She had thanked him sincerely. 'You are being so very kind and you have done so much already. . .there's no need of a nurse; if you don't mind, I'd like to be with Henry, just in case he wakes up during the night.'

He had nodded without comment and opened the door for her. She remembered how the beauty of the room had struck her and the feeling of gratitude towards Fulk for not dismissing Henry as just another little boy, prone to clumsiness and a little careless, but had considered him worthy of such handsome surroundings. But she had barely glanced at the blue and white tiled chimneypiece, the massive pillow cupboard, the tallboy and the little games table with the half-finished jigsaw puzzle on it, her eyes had flown to the narrow bed with its carved headboard and blue counterpane. Henry had looked very small and white lying there. She could hardly remember speaking to the nurse, who smiled and shook hands; she had gone at once to the chair drawn up to the bedside and sat down in it and taken her brother's hot little paw in her own hands. He had opened his eyes and said in a thread of a voice: 'Eleanor—Fulk said he'd fetch you. I'll go to sleep now.'

She had stayed quietly there while Fulk took the nurse down to her supper with Margaret and himself, promising that he would be back very shortly. 'I'm quite all right,' she had assured him, longing for a cup of tea.

He had smiled then. 'At least let me take your coat,' he suggested, 'and do be a sensible girl; you will be in and out of this room all night unless I am much mistaken, and if you don't eat you will be fit for nothing.'

He had been right, of course. He had come back surprisingly quickly and taken her place by the sleeping boy, urging her not to hurry: 'And if Henry wakes,' he had promised, 'I'll tell him you're at supper. Margaret is in her room—the second door facing the stairs— one of the maids is unpacking for her. I expect you would like to say goodnight to her.' He sat down and picked up a book and Eleanor, feeling herself dismissed, went out of the room.

Margaret, much refreshed by her supper, was disposed to be excited. 'Only imagine, a maid to unpack,' she told Eleanor, 'and there's a bathroom, all for me, and look at this room, isn't it sweet?'

It was indeed charming, pink and white and flowery with its white-painted furniture and chintz roses scattered over the curtains. Eleanor had admired it, kissed her sister goodnight and gone downstairs, where she found the housekeeper hovering in the hall, ready to lead her to her supper, a meal taken in another vast room, furnished with graceful mahogany pieces which could have been Sheraton. She had eaten her way through soup, ham soufflé, light as air, and baked apples smothered in cream and had been happily surprised when Juffrouw Witsma, looking a little puzzled, brought in a tea tray and set it before her. She went back upstairs presently, feeling a good deal better both in self and in temper, and Fulk must have seen it, for he said at once: 'That's better. Did you get your tea?'

Eleanor had beamed widely at him. 'Oh, yes, thank you. Do you drink tea in the evening here—with your supper, I mean?'

His mouth had twitched, but she hadn't seen it. 'Well, no, but I thought that you might like it.'

She had told him that he was most thought-ful and he had said smoothly: 'Oh, there's a

streak of good in every villain, you know,'
and gone on to speak of Henry and his treatment. 'He's very slightly better, I fancy. It's
a question of nursing and keeping him at rest
while the antibiotics get to work.' He walked
to the door. 'There's a bell by the bed, you
have only to ring.' He had gone before she
could utter a word.

Eleanor shook her head free of her
thoughts and glanced at the clock again, a
splendid cartel model in bronze. It was well
after midnight and Fulk hadn't returned,
although he had said that he would. She considered unpacking and getting ready for bed
and then returning to her chair; she could
doze well enough in it—she would give
Fulk another half hour, she decided, just
as he opened the door and came quietly
towards her.

He studied the chart she offered him, cast
an eye over the child and said reassuringly:
'Never mind the temperature, it should settle
in a day or two. I've telephoned the Manse
to let them know we've arrived safely—they
send you their love. Now go and have your
bath and get ready for bed, I'll sit here in the
meantime—I've some writing to do.'

There seemed no point in arguing; she
went to her room and looked around her.
Someone had unpacked her things; her

nightie and dressing gown had been carefully arranged on a chair, her slippers beside it. The bed, a delicate rosewood affair canopied in pale pink silk, had been turned down and the pink-shaded lights on the bedside tables switched on. It was a lovely room, its dressing table and tallboy matching the rosewood of the bed, its gilded mirrors and chintz-covered chairs giving it an air of luxury. Eleanor kicked off her shoes and, her tired feet inches deep in carpet, went to investigate the various doors. A cupboard, a vast one, handsomely equipped with lights and drawers and shelves so that her own few bits and pieces looked quite lost in it; and then a bathroom, small and pink and gleaming, with an extravagant supply of towels and soaps and bath luxuries to make her eyes sparkle. She ran a bath, dithered blissfully between Christian Dior and Elizabeth Arden and rushed out of her clothes; she would allow herself ten minutes.

It was a little longer than that before she went back to Henry's room, swathed in her blue quilted dressing gown, her hair plaited carelessly. Fulk stood up as she went in, casting her the briefest of glances as he busied himself collecting his papers.

'My room is at the front of the house, in the centre of the gallery,' he told her. 'If you want help, don't hesitate to call me—in any case I shall look in early in the morning, and we can discuss things then. He still has two more days on antibiotics, it's a question of patience.'

Eleanor nodded, fighting down an urge to cast herself on to his shoulder and burst into tears, something she felt he would dislike very much. When she had been a little girl, he had frequently called her a watering pot and she had no intention of giving him the chance to do so again. So she wished him a calm goodnight and took up her position by Henry's bed once more.

He wakened several times during the next few hours, staring at her with round hollow eyes, obediently swallowing his medicine, taking the drink she offered, but about three o'clock he fell into a more natural sleep, and presently, despite her efforts not to do so, Eleanor fell asleep too. She wakened two hours later; Henry was still sleeping and Fulk, in a dressing gown of great magnificence, was standing on the other side of the bed, looking at her. She struggled to get rid of the sleep fogging her head and mumbled apologetically: 'I must have dropped off—it was three o'clock. . .'

'Go to bed,' Fulk urged her with an impersonal kindness which nonetheless brooked no refusal. 'I'll stay here for an hour or so.'

She yawned widely. Bed would be heaven and with Fulk here to look after Henry, she knew that she would sleep, but she said at once: 'No, I can't do that; you have to go to Groningen in the morning—you said so.'

'I can go later.' He dismissed the matter. 'Do as I say, Eleanor—you'll be of no use to anyone as you are.'

Not perhaps the kindest way of putting it, but true, nevertheless. She got to her feet and said uncertainly: 'Very well, but you will call me? If I could just sleep for a couple of hours. . .'

He hadn't moved from the bed, he didn't look at her either, only said softly: 'Of course you will be called,' and bent over Henry.

She trailed off into the bedroom, her anxious mind full of the possibility of Henry's heart being damaged by his illness, so tired that she couldn't think about it properly any more. Her thoughts became a jumble of ward jobs she might have left undone before she left, her mother's worried letter, the fact that she had forgotten to bring any handkerchiefs with her, Miss Tremble's diet, which really didn't matter anyway, Henry's small white face and Fulk, popping up over and over again. She was wondering about that when she fell asleep.

CHAPTER SIX

ELEANOR wakened to find a fresh-faced young girl by her bed, holding a tray. She smiled when Eleanor sat up, put the tray on her knees, went to open the long brocade curtains, saying something friendly in a soft voice as she did so, and went away.

Eleanor shook the last wisps of sleep from her head, registered that it was light and morning, even if a grey one, and saw that the little Sèvres clock on the table beside her showed the hour to be half past eight.

She bounced out of bed and, dressing gown askew, no slippers on her feet, tore silently into the next room. Fulk was exactly as she had left him, the sheets of closely written paper scattered round his chair bearing testimony to his industry. There was a tray of coffee on the small table drawn up beside him; fragrant steam rose from the cup he was about to pick up. Henry was asleep.

Fulk raised his head and looked at her; at any other time she would have been furious at the mocking tilt of his eyebrows, but now she had other things on her mind. 'Why

124

didn't you call me?' she demanded in a whispered hiss.

The eyebrows expressed surprise as well as mockery. 'Did Tekla not bring you your breakfast? I asked her to do so.'

'Yes, she did.' She added a belated thank you. 'But it's half past eight.' She paused to survey him; he looked tired, but perhaps that was due to his unshaven chin and all the writing he had done. 'You have to go to Groningen,' she reminded him.

'How tedious that remark is becoming, Eleanor.' His voice was tolerant but his eyes still mocked her. 'I'm quite capable of organising my own day without your help, you know, and in any case at the moment you are being nothing but a hindrance. Go and eat your breakfast and put some clothes on.' The glance he gave her left her in no doubt as to what he thought of her appearance. 'You can have half an hour.'

He began to write once more, pausing only to add: 'Henry has slept soundly. We will discuss his treatment before I leave the house.'

She looked at him blankly, realizing dimly at that moment that her childish opinion of him had undergone a change, which considering his arrogant manner towards her was a little bewildering. She bit her lip and drew in her breath like a hurt child, murmured incoherently and turned on her heel. Fulk reached the door a second or so before she did and caught her by the shoulders. 'Why do you have to look like that?' he asked her harshly, and when she asked: 'Like what?', he went on: 'Like you used to when I wouldn't let you climb trees.' He gave her a little shake. 'I never thought. . .' he began, then went on in quite a different voice: 'I'm sorry, Eleanor—I had no right to speak to you like that. You've been wonderful—I whisked you away with no warning and then allowed you to sit here all night.' He bent and kissed her cheek gently. 'Now go and dress and eat your breakfast—please, Eleanor.'

She smiled then. 'You must be tired too, and you've a day's work before you. You've been so kind, Fulk—I keep saying that, don't I? but I can never thank you enough.' She added shyly: 'You've changed.'

'We have both changed—no, that's not right, you've not changed at all.'

Refreshed by a hasty breakfast, she bathed and dressed in a russet skirt and sweater, piled her hair neatly, and went back to Henry's room. Fulk was waiting for her. 'I'll be back within half an hour,' he told her from the door, and then: 'You haven't made up your face, it looks nice like that.'

She was left staring at the closing door, but only for a moment, for Henry opened his eyes at that moment and said in a wispy voice: 'Gosh, I'm thirsty.'

She gave him a drink, persuaded him to take his medicine, took his temperature and pulse, and washed his face and hands. 'And later on,' she told him firmly, 'after Fulk has been to see you, I shall give you a bedbath and change the sheets, and then you'll have another nice nap before lunch. Do you ache, my dear?'

Henry nodded. 'A bit, but I feel better, I think. When is Fulk coming?'

'Very soon—he's been sitting here for these last few hours while I had a sleep. He has to go to the hospital this morning.'

Henry closed his eyes, 'He's super,' he mumbled, 'I shall certainly be a doctor when I'm a man, I'm quite certain of that now—I shall be like Fulk; very clever and kind.'

'Yes, dear.' She smiled at him. 'Now stick out your tongue and I'll clean it for you. No, you can't do it; I'm sure Fulk has told you that you will get well much more quickly if you just lie still. I know it's a dead bore, but in a few days you'll be able to sit up. Shall I tell you a secret? Margaret came with us, she's coming to see you presently, and when you're better she'll be able to play cards with you.'

Henry smiled. 'Smashing—and will you read to me, too?'

'Certainly. Are there any English books here?'

'Dozens and dozens, they're in the library downstairs. Fulk lets me go there whenever I want, just so long as I put the books back again. He bought some in Groningen for me, too.'

'Splendid, we'll go through them together later. Now you're going to drink your milk, my dear.'

Fulk came back a few minutes later. Immaculately dressed, freshly shaved, he showed no sign of tiredness. His manner was friendly as he checked his small patient's pulse, gently examined him and pronounced himself satisfied. 'Two more days of antibiotics,' he stated, 'and by then you will be feeling much better, but that won't mean that you can get up, because you can't—it's important that you rest even if you think it a waste of time, so you will do exactly what Eleanor tells you—you understand that, old chap?'

He glanced at Eleanor, who murmured agreement; antibiotics might bring about a wonderful improvement in rheumatic fever;

they also caused the patient to feel so well that there was a danger of him getting up too soon and doing far too much, and that would do his heart no good at all.

'Why?' asked Henry.

The big man eyed the small boy thoughtfully. 'Since you are going to be a doctor one day, you are quite entitled to know the reasons for lying still and having everything done for you. I will explain them to you, but not now, for it would take quite a long time and I haven't even five minutes—I'm due at the hospital.' He grinned cheerfully at the white face on the pillow, barely glancing at Eleanor as he wished them *tot ziens*. She supposed that she had been included in his farewell, even if with such unflattering casualness, and her own 'goodbye' was cool. She took care not to watch him as he left the room too, so that it was all the more vexing when he popped his handsome head round the door again and found her gaze fixed upon it.

'You'll need some time off,' he reminded her. 'If you agree, Margaret could sit with Henry for an hour and certainly while you have your meals—she's a sensible child, isn't she?' He smiled at her suddenly. 'Why were you looking like that?' he asked.

'Like what?'

'Disappointed—bewildered—wistful, I'm not sure which. Never mind, I'll find out some time.' He had gone, and this time he didn't come back.

The day passed slowly. There wasn't a great deal for Eleanor to do, but Henry, normally the best-tempered child in the world, was rendered querulous by his illness, so that she was constantly occupied with him. It was only after he had fallen into an uneasy sleep in the early afternoon that she felt free to ring the bell and ask for Margaret to take her place while she ate her lunch; there would be no question of her taking time off; it wouldn't be fair on Margaret to leave her for more than a short time with her brother. Eleanor whispered instructions to her young sister and slipped from the room, to make her way downstairs to where her belated lunch was to be served in a small room behind the dining room in which she had had her supper on the previous evening. It was a cheerful apartment, with an open fire, a circular table accommodating six chairs, a mahogany side-table, beautifully inlaid, and a bow-fronted cabinet with a fluted canopy, its panels delicately painted. There was a tapestry carpet on the polished floor and the white damask cloth and shining silver and glass made the table very inviting. She sat down, apologising in English for her lateness, an apology which Juffrouw Witsma waved aside with nods and smiles and a gentle flow of soothing words which, while making no sense at all to Eleanor, nevertheless conveyed the assurance that coming down late to lunch was a trifling matter which wasn't of the least consequence.

The fresh-faced girl, Tekla, served her with a thick, delicious soup and then bore the plate away to return with a tray laden with a covered dish, a nicely arranged assortment of breads, cheeses and cold meats and a pot of coffee. The covered dish, upon investigation, contained an omelette which Eleanor devoured with a healthy appetite before pouring her coffee from the beautiful old silver coffee pot, and while she sipped the delicious brew from a delicate porcelain cup, she couldn't help but reflect upon the splendid style in which Fulk lived. Imogen was a lucky girl—that was, Eleanor reminded herself hastily, if she could put up with his occasional arrogance and his nasty habit of ignoring other people's remarks when he wished, although it wasn't likely that he would ignore Imogen. She switched her thoughts rather hastily, because for some reason or other she found that she didn't want to think about her.

She finished her meal quickly, not wanting to be away too long from Henry, and besides, she still had to go to the library and find a book so that when the invalid wakened presently she could read aloud to him.

There were a number of doors and several passages leading from the hall. She ignored the sitting room and the archway beside the staircase because it obviously led to the kitchen, and tried the door across the hall— Fulk's study; she cast an interested eye over the heavy masculine furniture, the enormous desk with its high-backed chair, the equally large wing chair drawn up to the old-fashioned stove, and the one or two rather sombre portraits on the panelled walls, and then shut the door again, wishing very much to stay and examine the room inch by inch.

She tried the big arched double doors next, facing the sitting room. This, then, was the library; she sighed with pleasure at the sight of so many books ranged on the shelves, the gallery running round the upper walls, and the little spiral staircase leading to it. There were two solid tables too with well upholstered leather chairs drawn up to them and reading lamps conveniently placed. She wandered round, wanting to pull out a handful of books and sit there and browse through them, but that wouldn't do at all; she glanced at her watch and quickened her steps, examining the shelves as she went. Henry had been right, there were quite a few children's books; she selected two or three and hurried back upstairs.

Henry was still asleep. Eleanor went over to where Margaret was perched anxiously by the bed and thanked her warmly. 'Darling, what are you going to do now?' she asked. 'You're not bored?'

Her sister shook her head. 'My goodness, no! Fulk telephoned someone he knew who has a daughter as old as I am, and she's coming over to spend the afternoon. Her name's Hermina and she speaks a little English.' She added seriously: 'Will you be all right if we go into the gardens for a walk?'

Eleanor glanced outside. It was a grey afternoon, but dry. 'Yes, love, but let me know when you come back, won't you? Is Hermina staying for tea?'

'Yes. Fulk said he'd be home for tea, too—but he's got to go out this evening.'

Evidently he preferred to share his plans with Margaret, thought Eleanor huffily, and then felt ashamed of the thought because he had been so kind to them all. She kissed her sister gently and took her place by the bed, and when she had gone, whiled away the time until he woke up, hot and cross and in a good deal of pain, by leafing through the books she had brought from the library: *Moonfleet*, *Treasure Island* and *The Wind in the Willows*. On the front page of each Fulk had written his name in a neat, childish hand, very much at variance with the fearful scrawl in which he had written Henry's notes.

She bathed Henry's hot face and hands, gave him a cooling drink and coaxed him to take his medicine. His temperature was still far too high, she noted worriedly, but took comfort from the fact that the antibiotics still had two days to go. She sat down again, picked up *The Wind in the Willows* and began to read aloud, stopping after half an hour to turn on the lamp and glance at the clock. Henry was lying quietly, listening to her placid reading, feeling for the moment a little better. She read on, with short intervals for him to have a drink, aware of a longing for a cup of tea herself. She embarked on chapter three, telling herself that Margaret would be along at any moment now.

But when the door eventually opened it was Fulk, not Margaret, who came in. He said hullo in a quiet voice and went at once to Henry, and only when he had satisfied himself that the boy was no worse he said:

'There is tea for you in the sitting room, Eleanor. The little girls are just finishing theirs, but Juffrouw Witsma will make you a fresh pot.'

'What about you?'

'I? I shall sit here with Henry.'

'Your tea?'

His voice held faint impatience. 'I had tea at the hospital.' He went to the door and held it open for her, and she found herself going across the wide gallery and down the stair-case without having said a single word.

Margaret jumped up as she went into the sitting room. 'I was just coming to you when Fulk came home,' she explained, 'and he said he was going to sit with Henry while you came down to tea—you don't mind, Eleanor?'

'Not a bit.' Eleanor glanced at the girl standing beside her sister and smiled. 'Is this Hermina?' she wanted to know as she shook hands. The girl was pretty, with pale hair and blue eyes and a wide smile; excellent company for Margaret, and how thoughtful of Fulk. . . She frowned, remembering how impatient he had been with her only a few minutes ago.

She poured herself a cup of tea from the little silver pot Juffrouw Witsma had set beside her and bit into a finger of toast. The two girls had wandered off to start a game of cards at the other end of the room, and she was left alone with her thoughts. But they were small comfort to her, what with Henry so poorly and Fulk treating her as though she were an evil necessity in his house—and yet upon occasion he had been rather nice. . . She poured herself another cup of tea, ate a piece of cake and went back upstairs.

'There wasn't all that hurry,' observed Fulk from his chair. He closed a folder full of notes as he spoke and got to his feet. 'Go and get your coat and take a brisk walk outside—the gardens are quite large.'

'I don't want. . .' began Eleanor, and caught his eye. 'Very well, but can you spare the time? Margaret could come. . .'

He sighed. 'I have the time,' he told her in a patient voice which made her grit her teeth. 'I wouldn't have suggested it otherwise. I have asked Juffrouw Witsma to sit here while you have dinner this evening, otherwise arrange things to suit yourself, but you must have exercise.' He picked up a book and sat down again. 'I shall be out.'

'Where?' asked Henry unexpectedly.

'That's rude, Henry,' Eleanor pointed out. 'You mustn't ask those sort of questions.'

Fulk cast down his book and strolled over to the bed. 'Hullo, boy—you're better—not well, but better. All the same, you will go on lying here doing nothing until I say otherwise.' He glanced quickly at Eleanor and addressed the boy. 'I'm going out to dine.'

'Who with?'

'Henry!' said Eleanor, mildly admonishing.

'Imogen's parents.'

'The lady you're going to marry?'

Fulk only smiled and the boy went on: 'Are they nice? As nice as Mummy and Daddy?'

Fulk thought for a moment. 'They're charming; their home is well ordered and they know all the right people.'

'Is it a big house? As big as this one?'

'Not quite as big.'

'I like your house,' his patient informed him seriously, 'but I like my home too, though I expect you find it rather small. Does the lady you're going to visit cook the dinner?'

The big man's mouth twitched as though he were enjoying a private joke. 'No, never. Now, your mother is a splendid cook, and even though your home is small it's one of the nicest houses I've been in.'

Henry beamed at him rather tiredly. 'Yes, isn't it—though I expect you'd rather live here.'

'Well, it is my home, isn't it?' He turned to Eleanor. 'Supposing you telephone your mother and father before you settle down for the evening? Tell them that this young man is picking up nicely and if he's as good tomorrow as he's been today, we'll bring the telephone up here and he can speak to them himself.'

'Oh, you really are super!' Henry declared, and fell instantly asleep.

Fulk went back to his chair. 'Well, run along, Eleanor.' He glanced at the slim gold watch on his wrist and smiled in casual, friendly dismissal, so that she went to her room without saying anything, put on her coat, snatched up her headscarf and mitts and went crossly downstairs. As soon as Henry was fit to be moved, she promised herself rashly, she would take him home, not bothering to go into the difficulties of such an undertaking. Not for the first time, she wondered why Fulk had bothered to bring her over to his home; Henry's persuasive powers, most likely, certainly not from his own wish.

It was cold and almost dark outside, with a starry, frosty sky and a cold moon which lighted her path for her. She walked briskly right round the house along the gravel drive which surrounded it and then down to the gates and back again. The house, now that she had the time to look at it properly in the moonlight, was even bigger than she had at first thought; she stood still, trying to imagine what it would be like to live in it and have it for a home, and while she stood there she heard a dog barking and remembered that she hadn't yet seen the dog Henry had mentioned, nor for that matter had she seen Moggy. She went indoors and poked her head round the sitting room door, where the girls were still playing cards.

'Have you seen Fulk's dog?' she asked her sister.

'Oh, yes—he's an Irish wolfhound, his name's Patrick O'Flanelly, but Fulk calls him Flan. Henry's kitten is here too—he's over here in the corner.'

She led the way to the other end of the room where Moggy lay sleeping in an old shopping basket lined with a blanket. 'Flan goes everywhere with Fulk, you know, he's in the kitchen now, having his supper, do you want to see him?'

'Yes, I'd love to, but not now, I'm going back to sit with Henry.'

Margaret slid a hand into hers. 'Fulk says Henry's better and that in a few days he'll be able to sit up and play some games with me. Are you going to telephone home? The place you have to call is here by the telephone—Fulk left it for you.'

He might get impatient with her, but he

wasn't to be faulted when it came to making things easy for her. She dialled the overseas exchange and a few minutes later heard her mother's voice.

'Henry's better,' she said at once because she knew that that was what her mother wanted to hear, and went on to reassure her before handing the telephone over to Margaret and hurrying back upstairs; it would never do for Fulk to be late for his dinner engagement.

It seemed very quiet after he had told her what to do for Henry, said a brief goodnight and gone away without a backward glance, indeed, she had the impression that he was glad to be going. Her brother was drowsing and she sat tiredly, hardly thinking, waiting for him to wake up so that she could do the variety of chores necessary for his quiet night, and if his temperature was down, she promised herself, and he seemed really better, she would get ready for bed and then sit with him until he fell asleep and then go to bed herself. She yawned widely at the very thought, then got up to study her brother's sleeping face; he did look better, and Fulk had said that he was, and she was quite sure that he would never have gone out for the evening unless he had felt easy in his mind about the boy.

It struck her all at once that she had no idea where Fulk had gone; she would have to go downstairs and find out, she was actually on her way to the door when her eye lighted on a fold of paper tucked into *The Wind in the Willows*. It was a note, brief and to the point, telling her that should she need Fulk, he could be reached at a Groningen number. 'The Atlanta Hotel,' he had scrawled. 'Don't hesitate to let me know if you are worried. If I have left the hotel, try this number.' He had printed it very clearly so that she could make no mistake. She read the businesslike missive through once more, wondering whose the second number was; not the hospital, she knew that already. She told herself sharply not to be nosey.

It was past midnight before Henry finally fell into a quiet sleep. Margaret had tiptoed in to say goodnight hours before; Eleanor decided to have her bath and get ready for bed, something which she did speedily, with the door open so that she might hear the slightest sound, but Henry slept on, with none of the restless mutterings and tossing and turning of the previous night. She glanced at the small enamel clock on the dressing table, decided that she would read until one o'clock and went back to her chair once more; she should have chosen a book for herself while she had been in the library; now she would have to content herself with *The Wind in the Willows*, a book she had read many times already. She settled down to enjoy Toad's activities.

The clock's silvery chimes recalled her to the time. She looked once more at Henry, sleeping peacefully, yawned widely and then gave a choking gasp as Fulk said from the door: 'Still up? There's no need tonight, you know—he's better.'

She peeped at him through the curtain of hair she hadn't bothered to plait. He was leaning against the door jamb, his hands in the pockets of his exquisitely tailored dinner jacket; elegant and self-assured and not over-friendly. She wondered why. Perhaps dining with Imogen's parents had filled his mind with thoughts of her, and coming back to herself, sitting untidily wrapped in a dressing gown and her hair anyhow, could be irritating to him. She said apologetically: 'I know—I'm going to bed now; I've been reading and I forgot the time.'

He came across the room and took the book from her knee. 'Well, well,' his eye-brows rose an inch, 'bedtime stories. A little old for Toad, aren't you, Eleanor?'

'I've been reading it to Henry,' she snapped, 'and I don't see what age has to do with it, anyway,' she said pointedly: 'It's your book.'

He was leafing through it. 'Yes, but I fancy I've outgrown it.'

'And that's a pity, though from what I remember of you, you probably didn't enjoy it when you were a little boy.'

He grinned at her. 'Meaning that even at an early age I had already formed my regrettable character?'

She remembered the trouble he had taken over Henry, and how he had gone to the rescue of the children on that snowy afternoon, and was filled with contrition. 'Oh, Fulk, I didn't mean that, really I didn't. I suppose I'm tired and my tongue's too sharp—and how could we possibly agree about anything?'

He put the book down. 'Now, why not?'

'Well, we don't lead the same kind of life, do we? All this. . .?' She waved a hand at the luxurious room. 'And me—I like sitting in the loft at home with Mrs Trot. . .' It sounded very silly when she had said it, and she wasn't looking at him, so she didn't see his smile.

'One can have the best of both worlds,' he observed blandly.

'Now what on earth do you mean by that?' she demanded in a whisper.

'Never mind now. Has Henry slept all the evening?'

'Yes, and so restfully too. Do you suppose he'll wake before morning?'

'Unlikely—the antibiotics have taken effect; he'll feel fighting fit in the morning and it will take our united efforts to keep him quiet in bed.'

She fetched a small sigh. 'It's such a load off my mind—we all love him very much, you see. I'll never be able to thank you enough for all you've done.'

'I may take you up on that one day.' He bent and kissed her cheek lightly. 'Now let us examine these charts.'

He studied her carefully kept records, took Henry's pulse, used his stethoscope on the small sleeping chest, expressed satisfaction at his findings, and went to the door. 'With care he'll do, and no after-effects, either.'

His smile was so kind that she found herself saying: 'What a dear you are! I do hope you had a pleasant evening; I don't suppose you get out much.'

'Er—no—not when Imogen is away. The evening was pleasant enough. Imogen's mother was interested to hear about Henry and sends her good wishes for his speedy recovery.'

'How very kind of her.' She was laying

the charts tidily on the table. 'You must miss Imogen very much.'

He didn't answer her, merely wished her goodnight and closed the door soundlessly. If she hadn't been so tired she might have wondered at that. As it was she took a final look at her small brother and went thankfully to her bed.

CHAPTER SEVEN

FULK had been quite right; Henry wakened in the morning feeling so much more himself that he wanted to get up; Eleanor was arguing gently with him about it when Fulk walked in and said at once: 'Ah, good——I see that you are on the road to recovery, boy. Eleanor, go and have your breakfast while I explain to Henry just why he has to stay quietly in bed for a little longer.' He glanced at her. 'You slept? Good. I’ve had breakfast and I don’t need to leave the house for an hour, so don’t hurry back.' His smile dismissed her.

Margaret caught her up on the staircase and tucked a hand into hers. 'It’s all so grand,' she confided, 'but Fulk doesn’t seem to notice it, does he?'

'Well, I suppose when you’ve lived in a place like this all your life, it’s as much home to him as the Manse is to us, dear.'

'Fulk says Henry’s better, he says that if I ask you nicely you might let me come and talk to Henry later on. May I?'

They had reached the small room where they had their breakfast and sat down at the table, essayed a '*Goeden morgen,*' to Tekla and made much of Flan who had joined them silently. Margaret offered him a piece of toast and said: 'I went to see Moggy just now, he's in the kitchen with Juffrouw Witsma—he likes her cat, you know, but he had his breakfast here with Fulk, he always does.'

Eleanor was conscious of surprise; Fulk was a busy man and yet he hadn't just consigned Moggy to the care of his housekeeper, he had offered him companionship as well. She hadn't expected it. 'Does he?' she commented, 'how nice.' Fulk had qualities she hadn't suspected. 'He doesn't have much time. . .'

Margaret slipped Flan some more toast. 'No, he doesn't, does he? But when he comes home in the evening he always fetches Moggy to sit with him. Flan sits with him too, of course.'

They ate their breakfast without haste while they discussed various ways of amusing Henry during his convalescence. 'Cards,' declared Margaret emphatically, 'he loves playing cards.'

'As long as he doesn't get too excited. Draughts, too, and what about Ludo?'

Margaret curled her lip. 'Eleanor, that's a child's game!'

'But Henry's a child, dear.'

'Oh, I know that, but he's so bright for his age—why, he's been playing chess with Daddy ever since last winter.'

'Heavens! What about Monopoly? That's a good game, but he might get too excited. Anyway, I'll ask Fulk.'

But there was no opportunity to do that when she went back upstairs. Fulk had resumed his role of doctor again, and beyond giving her his precise instructions about her brother, he had nothing more to say, indeed, his very manner discouraged her from anything but a meek: 'Yes, Fulk, no, Fulk,' in answer.

The day passed without incident, and Henry was so much improved by the afternoon that Eleanor felt justified in allowing Margaret to sit with him for a brief while, so that she might take a brisk walk in the gardens. They were larger than she had thought and in excellent order. She poked around, exploring paths and examining the variety of shrubs and trees bordering them, and it was quite half an hour before she returned to the house, to find a Mercedes outside the front door; it was a 450SE, and a new model, all gleaming coachwork and chromium. It looked a little vulgar. Perhaps it belonged to Hermina's father, although Eleanor couldn't remember Margaret saying that her new friend would be coming that afternoon. She mounted the steps, pausing in the vestibule to take off her boots, for she had got them muddy at the edge of the pond she had discovered behind the house, and it would never do to sully the shining floors. She tugged off her headscarf, pulling her hair askew as she did so, and with the boots dangling from one hand, opened the inner door and started for the stairs. She had a stockinged foot on the lowest tread when the drawing room door opened and a woman came out and stood looking at her.

She was of middle age, handsome in a large way and dressed with taste and, Eleanor guessed, great expense. Her voice, when she spoke, was commanding and her English, although fluent, was heavily accented.

'You are the nurse?' She sounded surprised too, which wasn't to be wondered at, thought Eleanor reasonably; the word hardly conjured up a windswept hairdo, stockinged feet and muddy boots dangling. . .

She said: 'Yes, I am. Did you want me?'

The lady advanced a foot or two. 'Do you know who I am?' she enquired.

'I'm afraid I don't—ought I to?' Eleanor hoped her voice didn't betray her growing dislike of her interrogator.

'Did the professor not tell you?'

'The professor? Who's he?. . .oh, you mean Fulk.' Eleanor smiled and met a stony stare.

'I,' said the lady weightily, 'am the professor's future mother-in-law.'

Eleanor stopped herself just in time from saying 'Poor Fulk', and murmured a polite how do you do instead. Surely Imogen wasn't like this dreadful woman——Fulk must love her very much to be able to put up with her mother. She said, still polite: 'It was kind of you to enquire about my brother——he's better today; we're all very relieved.'

Imogen's mother inclined her severely coiffured head graciously. 'I am glad to hear it. I must say that you are hardly what I imagined you to be.' Her cold eyes swept over Eleanor's somewhat tatty person, so that she felt constrained to say: 'Oh, I look better in uniform——and now if you will excuse me I must go back to my brother. I expect you're waiting for Fulk?'

'No, nurse, I came to see you. As Imogen is not here, I felt it to be my duty. . .'

'To look me over and make sure that I wasn't getting my claws into Fulk?' asked Eleanor, quite forgetting her manners. 'Well, I daresay you feel better about it now——I'm not the glamorous type, you see——I just work for a living. Goodbye, Mevrouw. . .I don't know your name, I'm afraid.'

She started up the stairs and was brought to a halt by the commanding voice. 'Oss van Oss, Nurse, Baroness Oss van Oss—and you are quite correct. I can quite see now why Fulk is not in the least attracted to you—I am greatly reassured. I told him last night that I considered it a little irregular for you to be in his house, and I advised him to obtain one of the older nurses from his hospital in your place now that the little boy is no longer dangerously ill. I would not wish to influence him unduly, but I have dear Imogen's feelings to consider.'

Eleanor had swung round to face the Baroness. 'Can't she look after her own feelings?' she enquired pertly, and then: 'What a horrid conversation this is, isn't it? You might as well know that your daughter's feelings are of no importance to me, but my brother's health is. I shall stay here until he is better, and since, as you have just told me, Fulk isn't in the least attracted to me, I can't see what all the fuss is about. Goodbye, Baroness Oss—no, Oss van Oss, isn't it?'

She went on her way unhurriedly, aware that she was being stared at, and despite her deliberate step, she seethed with rage. How dared the woman come to look her over, and how dared Fulk allow it? She was just beginning to like him despite his offhand manner, now she found herself disliking him more than ever. She would have something to say when she saw him!

Which wasn't until much later, although he came in the early evening to see Henry; but he brought someone with him, an elderly man, who called Henry little man and herself dear lady, and muttered a good deal to himself. Fulk introduced him as Professor van Esbink, explaining that he had thought a second opinion of Henry's condition might reassure them all. Eleanor hadn't answered him and had given him a stony stare when he smiled at her, so that the smile turned into a mocking one before he turned away to answer his learned colleague's questions. Any other man might have been disconcerted, but Fulk wasn't like other men. She became very professional in her manner and when she saw the two gentlemen to the door, her manner was not only professional, it was glacial, at least towards Fulk.

'You've taken umbrage,' said Henry from his bed, and when, an hour later, Fulk came back he pointed this interesting fact out to the doctor. 'Eleanor is in a temper,' he said, 'and I don't know why.'

Fulk glanced across the room to where Eleanor was standing, measuring medicine into a glass. 'She's plain ratty,' he declared cheerfully, 'and I think I know why.'

'Why?' asked Henry with interest.

'Since I have no intention of telling you, I shouldn't waste time asking, boy. Let us concentrate instead on what Professor van Esbink had to say about you. He agrees with me that you are doing very nicely, but just as I explained to you, you still have to remain quietly in bed, though I think that Margaret might come and play some quiet game with you for a couple of hours each day, and I daresay Moggy would be glad to visit you.'

'Oh. I say—may he really come? on to my bed?'

'Why not? And certainly he may stay here as long as he likes. I daresay that once he has been shown the way, he'll pop in and out as the fancy takes him.' He smiled down at the boy. 'I'll go and find Margaret and ask her to bring him up here for a little while, shall I?'

He was back very soon with Margaret, clutching Moggy. The kitten was settled under Henry's hand, and his sister esconced in a chair by the bed. 'And no sitting up, Henry,' said Fulk firmly. 'Margaret, ring the bell if you should need us, I'm going to take Eleanor down to dinner.'

Eleanor cast him a look to freeze a man's bones, 'I am not hungry, thank you.'

He said nothing at all, merely crossed the room, took her by the arm and led her away, hurrying her down the staircase so fast that she had much ado not to trip up.

In the drawing room he shut the door behind them and invited her to sit down by the fire. 'And what would you like to drink?' he enquired solicitously. 'Not spirits, I think; they might only serve to inflame your temper even more. How about Madeira? Pleasantly alcoholic without clouding the mind.'

She accepted the glass he offered her, for there was really nothing else she could do about it. Besides, it gave her a few minutes in which to gather her thoughts; she had no wish to lose her temper; calm, cool, reasoning, with a slight hint of hurt feelings would fill the bill very well.

'I'm waiting for the outburst,' he prompted blandly, so that she was instantly possessed of a great desire to speak her mind. But she made a strong effort to keep her cool; her voice was mild as she said slowly:

'Your future mother-in-law came this afternoon, but I expect you know that already.'

'Juffrouw Witsma told me when I came in. I wondered if she would.'

Eleanor put her glass carefully down on the charming little lamp table at her elbow.

'You knew she was coming? To look me over? I cannot quite understand why you could not have reassured her sufficiently; it would have saved her a journey.' Her voice, despite her best efforts, became a little shrill. 'She was good enough to explain to me that as you were not in the least attracted to me she felt quite at ease about me, although she considered that I should be—removed. . .' She choked on rage. 'How dared you allow her. . .she's a detestable woman, and I have no intention of apologizing to you for saying so; it's to be hoped that your Imogen doesn't take after her.' Her wrathful voice petered out before the expression on Fulk's face, but it served to fan her temper at the same time. 'If I go, I shall take Henry too,' she told him flatly. 'I'll get an ambulance if it takes every penny I've got—and I hope I never, never see you again!'

She picked up her glass and was annoyed to find that her hand was trembling so that it was hard to hold it steady. Fulk must have seen it too, for he came over to her, took the glass from her and put it down again. 'A family heirloom,' he explained mildly. 'You know, Eleanor, it is a remarkable thing that you can stir up my deepest feelings with such ease; at one moment I am so angry with you that I could cheerfully wring your neck, and at the next I find abject apologies for my shocking behaviour tripping off my tongue. Of course I discussed you with Baroness Oss van Oss, but hardly in the manner which she implied—indeed, I imagined that she was joking when she said that she would like to meet you and see what you were like for herself, and when she persisted, I told her that I could see no reason why she shouldn't if she wished—I imagined that it would be a friendly visit, no more; I had no idea that she was going to upset you and I am deeply sorry for that. And as for all that nonsense about replacing you with another nurse, I have no intention of doing any such thing; you will remain until you are perfectly satisfied that Henry is well again.' He smiled wryly. 'You know, I have the strongest feeling that we should be laughing about the whole thing, enjoying the joke together. And here we are, quarrelling again.'

'People who don't like each other always quarrel,' said Eleanor, not bothering to look at him.

'Ah, yes—I was forgetting that you have a long-standing dislike of me; not even the common denominator of Henry's illness has altered that, has it?' He put her glass back into her hand. 'Drink up and we will go in to dinner. I'm hungry.'

It was disconcerting that, just when she was striving to reduce her rage to reasonable argument, he should dampen it down by wanting his dinner. She wasn't sure if she wanted to laugh about it or have a good cry.

She found herself in the dining room, facing him across the broad expanse of linen set with heavy old silver and delicate glass, and rather to her surprise she found that she was hungry too, and after a little while, enjoying herself. The food was delicious and Fulk's gentle flow of small talk was undemanding and mildly amusing. She studied his face as he bent to pull gently on one of Flan's ears—the dog was sitting like a statue beside his chair, watching him with adoring eyes. Fulk was smiling a little and she wondered if she had been mistaken at the expression on his face when she had mentioned Imogen. She still wasn't quite sure what it had been, only it had made her uncertain; perhaps she had been mistaken about him, too—perhaps all her ideas about him had been wrong. It was an ever-recurring thought which refused to be dispelled, and the memory of her strongly voiced wish never to see him again struck her so forcibly that she put down her spoon and stared at the contents of her plate, wondering what she should do about it.

'Don't you like caramel custard?' asked Fulk. 'I'll ring and get Juffrouw Witsma to bring something else.'

Eleanor transferred her gaze from her plate to his face. 'I like it very much, thank you.' She went on quite humbly: 'Fulk, I'm sorry I was so rude just now—about Baroness Oss van Oss, I mean. I had no right to speak like that and I'm sure your Imogen is the nicest and most beautiful girl in the world, and if you want to discuss me with anyone, I—I really don't mind; I'm only the nurse, after all, and I don't care about anything except getting Henry well again so that he'll grow up strong and healthy.'

He got up and came round the table to sit carelessly on it beside her so that he could look down into her face. 'My dear Eleanor,' he begged, 'for heaven's sake don't talk like that, it just isn't you—so meek and penitent. And you're not "only the nurse",' he paused, his dark eyes looking over her head, 'you are a great many things. . .' His sombre expression was gone, he grinned at her. 'Shall we telephone your people before we go upstairs?'

Henry had a relapse the next day; not a severe one but sufficient to delay his convalescence. Eleanor, looking back on those few days when they were happily past, wondered

how she would have got through them without Fulk's help. Henry had been querulous
and difficult and the very mention of another
nurse coming to relieve Eleanor caused him
to toss and turn in such a frenzy of unrest
that the idea was given up and Fulk took
turns with Eleanor in nursing him, something
which he did with no fuss at all, apparently
being quite able to work at his consulting
rooms and the hospital by day, and sit up for
a good part of each night without any ill
effects.

Happily the relapse had been a brief one;
on the fourth day Henry had woken up with a
temperature which was almost normal again,
demanding tea and toast and Margaret to talk
to. Eleanor, hearing voices in her brother's
room at five o'clock in the morning, had gone
at once to see what the matter was, and discovered Fulk sitting back in his chair, sharing
a pot of tea with his patient. He had taken
one look at her distraught countenance and
said comfortably: 'Fetch a tooth mug,
Eleanor, and join us in our early tea; Henry
is debating the important question as to what
he would like for his breakfast. I fancy that
we are out of the wood.'

She had gone back into the bathroom and
picked up the mug and then sat down on the
edge of the bath. She had been wanting

to have a good cry for some time now, but somehow the opportunity had never occurred, but now, opportunity or not, the tears poured down her cheeks, willy-nilly. She hardly noticed when Fulk took the mug from her, wiped her face with a towel and sat down beside her. 'Watering pot,' he said kindly, 'you weep as copiously as you used to when you were a little girl.'

She sniffed into the towel. 'So would you if you were me,' she declared in a muffled voice. 'I've been so afraid that Henry...do you suppose there will be any lasting damage?'

'Unlikely.' Fulk had put an arm round her and it felt very comforting. 'This setback only means that he has to take a little longer to get on to his feet again.'

Eleanor sniffed. 'You're sure?' And then because of the look of surprise on his face: 'Oh, I do beg your pardon, just for a moment I forgot who you were—of course you're sure. How happy Mother and Father will be...' She sat up and felt his arm slacken. 'I'll get dressed and get some breakfast for Henry—shall I get some for you too? You've been sitting there since twelve o'clock, you must be hungry. If you're very quick, you could get at least three hours' sleep before you need to leave.'

'So I could, but I won't, I'll have breakfast with Henry and you. Scrambled eggs for him and weak tea, and I'll have eggs and bacon— three eggs, and toast and marmalade and coffee—you have whatever you like for yourself. Don't dress; if Henry has a light meal now he will probably sleep again for several hours and that will do him good as well as keep him quiet.' He studied her face. 'You don't look too bad,' he remarked. 'Off with you and I'll come down and carry the tray up for you—fifteen minutes, OK?'

'OK,' she smiled rather mistily, and went down to the kitchen, a vast room with a vaulted ceiling, cupboards which would have housed a family, an imposing dresser which took up the whole of one wall, and enough labour-saving gadgets to gladden the heart of the most pernickety woman—no wonder Juffrouw Witsma always looked so contented! Eleanor peered around her with envy and opened the nearest cupboard door.

Fulk had been right again; Henry ate every morsel of his frugal breakfast, murmured 'Super,' and went at once to sleep, not to wake again until the morning was far advanced, demanding something else to eat. And that evening when Fulk came home they all played a sedate game of Ludo, careful not to get too excited about it, and when finally

Henry had been tucked down for the night they went down to dinner, leaving Tekla on guard, because, as Fulk pointed out, she was a sensible girl with a string of small brothers and sisters of her own and knew how to handle children. Their meal was a cheerful one, for Margaret and Fulk were on excellent terms with each other and between them soon had Eleanor laughing with them.

The week passed quickly after that, with Henry improving rapidly—too rapidly, for he wanted to do everything at once. It was easier when at the end of the week, Fulk said that he might sit out for an hour or two each day, so that he and Margaret could amuse themselves at the small card table, and Eleanor seized these brief periods in which to take brisk walks, enjoying the wintry weather and the cold wind after so many days indoors. She ventured out of the grounds after the first day, exploring the narrow lanes running between the flat, frost-covered water meadows. There wasn't a great deal to see, but it was peaceful as well as invigorating. She told herself that she felt much better for these outings, while at the same time aware that there was a hard core of sadness somewhere deep inside her, which for some reason or other she was loath to probe.

She saw little of Fulk; he left early each

morning and sometimes he wasn't back until after they had had their dinner in the evening. He saw Henry twice a day, of course, but his remarks were mostly limited to the boy's condition, and recommendations as to his further treatment. Walking briskly back to the house on the Friday afternoon, Eleanor found herself looking forward to the week-end; Fulk would be home.

He arrived after tea, driving the Daimler Sovereign he used for the short journey to and from the hospital and his consulting rooms. Eleanor, who happened to be in the hall when he came in, thought that he looked tired and bad-tempered with it; he must have had a tiresome day. She said 'Hullo,' in a conciliatory voice and asked: 'Shall I ask someone to bring you some tea?'

He had shrugged himself out of his topcoat and started across the hall towards his study, his briefcase in his hand. 'No time,' he told her briefly, and went inside, closing the door firmly behind him. Eleanor went upstairs to make sure that Henry wasn't getting above himself, cautioned him in a sisterly fashion, bade Margaret keep a sharp eye on her brother and went downstairs again to look for Moggy. She was returning from the kitchen, the kitten tucked under one arm, when she encountered Fulk once more, and urged on by a wish to see his tired face smile, asked: 'Did you have a bad day?'

He checked his stride to look at her. He was in a bad temper all right, his dark face frowning, his mouth a straight line; it surprised her very much when he said: 'No,' but she waited a moment, thinking that he might want to say something else. When he did speak, she was even more surprised.

'I'm going away for the weekend,' he said in a bland, cold voice she didn't much care for. 'Henry's quite safe to leave; in any case, I've asked Professor van Esbink to keep an eye on him. I'm leaving in half an hour and when I return on Tuesday I shall go straight to my rooms, so if you wish to say anything, you had better say it now.'

Eleanor stood, her mouth a little open, quite unable to think of a single word to say. When he said, still in that hateful voice: 'You're not usually so short of words,' she snapped her mouth shut and then said:

'What am I supposed to say? I'll wish you a pleasant weekend if that's what you want, though in your present nasty temper I should be sorry for your companions, but perhaps you'll feel better by the time you get to wherever you're going.'

'Fishing!' he declared. 'You want to know

where I'm going, don't you? Cannes——to see Imogen.'

Eleanor was conscious of a peculiar sensation which she didn't have time to ponder. She said with false cheerfulness: 'How nice for you both,' and then more urgently: 'You're never going to drive all that way and then back again by Tuesday?'

He raised his brows. 'Why ever not?'

'It's miles—you're tired already. . .'

His voice was silky now. 'Eleanor, I brought you here to look after your brother. And now, if you will excuse me.'

'It's too far,' declared Eleanor wildly.

'Roughly seven hundred and fifty miles— fifteen hours' driving on excellent roads.' He smiled thinly. 'If it makes you feel better, I shall only drive six or seven hours before I rack up for the night. I should be in Cannes some time during tomorrow afternoon.'

'But coming back?' she persisted, and then drew a sharp breath as he said blandly: 'I haven't been so fussed over since I had a nanny.'

She stood just where she was, watching him go, listening to the high-powered whine of the Panther. It sounded very loud in the quiet house.

'Fuss over him!' said Eleanor to no one in particular. 'Of course I fuss over him, and how fantastic it is that I've only just this minute discovered that I'm in love with the wretch.' The sad feeling could be explained now, as well as the eager looking forward to the weekend; perhaps she had known all the time without realizing it.

She kissed the top of Moggy's furry little head and started slowly up the staircase; the less she thought about it the better; by the time she saw Fulk again on Tuesday she would have forced herself to accept the idea and turn her back on it—because that was what she was going to have to do. She allowed herself a few moments of pure envy of Imogen, wondering what it would be like to know that a man loved you so much that he would make a round trip of fifteen hundred miles just to be with you for a day. She sighed so deeply that Moggy became dislodged and stuck a needlelike claw into her arm; she didn't feel it, her thoughts were with Fulk, driving through the dark winter evening and on into an even darker night, intent on reaching his Imogen as quickly as possible.

Eleanor paused at the top of the stairs; if she had been Imogen she would have gone half way—no, the whole way, to meet Fulk. After all, the girl did nothing, while he was wearing himself to a shadow, what with his work at the hospital, his own practice, and staying up half the night with Henry. That there was something absurd in describing a large man of fifteen stone or thereabouts as being worn to a shadow didn't cross her mind. She could only imagine him going to sleep at the wheel of his powerful car and crashing somewhere remote and dying before anyone could reach him. She opened Henry's door, offered Moggy to her brother and allowed herself to be persuaded to enjoy a game of three-handed whist. She played very badly; understandable enough, considering that her head was full of Fulk and nothing else.

The weekend dragged by on leaden feet for Eleanor. Somehow she got through it, thankful that Henry was indeed well again and that Margaret was perfectly content to stay where she was. She telephoned her parents each evening because Fulk had told her to do so, giving them a racy account of Henry's progress and even venturing to speak of his return in the not too distant future. 'Perhaps for Christmas,' she essayed. 'I've not given a thought to presents yet, we're miles from the shops, you know, and I haven't been able to get out much—I'll have to rush round and buy them when we get back.' The thought of the ward and of

Miss Tremble, who would certainly be there, and all the rush and bustle of Christmas in hospital gave her no joy at all, and her feelings must have sounded in her voice, for her mother asked: 'You're all right, dear? You sound. . .perhaps you're tired.'

Eleanor agreed that she was and handed the receiver to Margaret.

It was late on Tuesday evening before she saw Fulk. It had been a cold day with a hint of snow. Probably it was this inclement weather as well as his long drive which had so lined and sharpened his handsome features. Henry had been asleep for some time and Margaret was flitting around in her dressing gown, putting off her own bedtime for as long as possible while Eleanor carried up the lemonade which Henry might want in the night before going downstairs once again to fetch Moggy to sleep on the end of the invalid's bed. She was on her way upstairs once more, the little beast under her arm, when the door behind her opened and shut, and when she turned round: 'How's Henry?' asked Fulk.

She saw his tired face. 'He's splendid. Professor van Esbink telephoned twice, but there was no need for him to come.'

Fulk threw his coat and gloves into a chair and crossed the hall to stand at the foot of the stairs. 'I know, he telephoned me this morning. He has a high opinion of you, Eleanor, did you know that? He would like you to work for him.'

She digested this flattering information in silence and jumped when he said sharply: 'Well, aren't you going to ask me if I had a pleasant weekend?'

'Well, I did want to,' she told him spiritedly, 'but I didn't feel like being snubbed.'

He moved very fast; he was beside her almost before she had finished speaking. She hadn't bargained for it and he was far too near for her peace of mind, and that peace was wholly shattered when he kissed her quite fiercely on her mouth, all without saying a word. He was back in the hall again while she was still blinking over it.

'I'm going to have something to eat,' he told her in a perfectly ordinary voice. 'I'll be up to see Henry later.'

CHAPTER EIGHT

FULK didn't come for almost an hour, which gave Eleanor time to find a number of good reasons for his behaviour. It had been a kind of reaction, she told herself; he had been with Imogen and probably he was missing her terribly, and because Eleanor had been the only girl around he had probably kissed her to relieve his unhappy feelings. It was a silly argument, but she couldn't think of a better one. The obvious thing to do was to ignore the whole incident, which wasn't very easy, but by the time he did appear, she had succeeded in acquiring a calm manner and a placid face, although beneath this exemplary façade her feelings were churning around inside her in a most disturbing manner.

But it had all been rather a waste of time, for he had barely looked at her and his manner, when he spoke, was very much that of the family doctor—affable, impersonal and just a little out of reach. He stayed only long enough to assure himself that all was well with Henry before wishing her a casual good night and going away again, and she went to bed shortly afterwards, quite bewildered and very unhappy.

Henry was allowed up the next day; dressed, he looked small and thin and far too pale, but his appetite was excellent and although his exercise was very limited, he was at least on his feet once more. The weather was still wintry, but Fulk, after the first couple of days, took him for short drives each day, fitting them in, Eleanor suspected, during his lunch hour, but when she had remonstrated about this, he had told her quite sharply that he had plenty of free time during the middle of the day and that he enjoyed the drives as much as his passenger did.

It would be Sint Nikolaas in a few days; Eleanor, who had heard all about it from Margaret, who had in her turn got it from Hermina, wondered if Fulk intended to do anything about it. She didn't like to bring the subject up in case he felt that she was expecting him to celebrate the occasion in some way, but on the other hand Margaret had told Henry about it and she had heard them speculating together as to whether they would be getting any presents; she would have to do something about it after all. Until this moment she hadn't needed any money; she had a little English money with her, but no Dutch, and it looked as though she would need some; she didn't like the idea, but she would have to talk to Fulk about it.

But there was no need; at breakfast the next morning, a meal at which she arrived a little late because of Henry's small demands, Margaret was already broaching the matter. Fulk, immersed in his mail, as he almost always was, got to his feet as she joined them, wished her good morning and went back to his letters. Eleanor didn't think that he looked over-friendly, but Margaret hadn't noticed his withdrawn expression, or if she had, she had decided to ignore it.

'Fulk,' she said cheerfully, 'I want to go to some shops and I expect Eleanor does too, only I don't know how to set about it. I haven't any money, though Eleanor has, but it's pounds. Could we leave Henry for just a little while, do you suppose?'

He put down the letter he was reading and gave her his full attention. 'My dear child, that can easily be arranged——how stupid of me not to have thought of it before.' He glanced at Eleanor, his eyebrows raised. 'Why did you not ask me sooner?'

'Well——I hadn't thought about it, not until yesterday, and I had no idea that Margaret was going to say anything to you——I'd made up my mind to ask you myself.'

'You should have asked sooner. I'm afraid

that I can't spare the time to stay with Henry, but I will arrange for a nurse to come for the day and keep him company—would tomorrow suit you?'

He smiled nicely at her, although she had the impression that his mind was occupied by some other matter. She said diffidently: 'Well, if it's not being too much of a bother. . .'

He was reading his letter again. 'None whatever,' he assured her. He got up to go very shortly afterwards, pausing only to say: 'Let me have what money you wish to change, Eleanor, and I will give you guldens for it.'

When he had gone Eleanor turned to her sister. 'Darling,' she cried, 'whatever made you ask Fulk? I mean, he was so preoccupied. I'd thought about it too, but really this morning of all times, when you could see that he had all those letters.'

'Pooh,' said Margaret forcefully, 'he'd read them all ages ago. He wasn't busy at all, just staring at that letter he was holding— he'd read it at least six times—I watched him. Besides, I want to buy Henry something for Sint Nikolaas, he'll be frightfully disappointed if he doesn't get a present. How shall we go? I suppose Groningen is the nearest place?'

'I should think so—perhaps there's a bus. I wonder if a taxi would cost a lot?' Eleanor frowned. 'And when are we to go? In the morning or after lunch, and do you suppose there will be someone in the shops who'll speak English?'

She worried about it on and off during the rest of the day, which turned out to be a waste of time, for when Fulk came home he told them that he would return during the midday break and drive them into Groningen and pick them up again when he had finished his work in the afternoon. 'Better still,' he suggested, 'I'll show you where my consulting rooms are and you can come there. Eleanor, if you will come with me, I'll give you the money you require.'

She fetched her purse and followed him across the hall to his study. 'I'm not sure how much we need to spend,' she told him. 'It's just a present for Henry, and I want to buy something for Margaret, too. . .'

He had gone to his desk and opened a drawer. 'How much money can you spare?' he asked her bluntly.

'Well, would ten pounds be enough?' It sounded a lot of money and they hadn't much to buy.

He had his head bent so that she couldn't see his face, he said gently: 'I daresay—all the same, supposing I let you have more than that; you can repay me later. I should perhaps have warned you that it is customary to give everyone a small gift on Sint Nikolaas Eve; perhaps you should buy some small trifle for Juffrouw Witsma and Tekla and Bep—oh, and old Mevrouw Brom, too.'

'Oh, yes, of course, if that's the thing to do. I thought it was just for children.'

She watched him counting out the notes, loving every dark hair on his head and every line on his good-looking face, and there were lines, she could see that; perhaps he was working too hard, that long journey to Cannes must have tired him out. She cried soundlessly: 'Oh, Fulk, why did you have to fall in love with the wrong girl?' and because he was holding the money out to her with thinly veiled impatience, took it from him, thanked him quietly and left him alone.

He had gone in the morning when she got down to breakfast. The nurse, a cheerful young girl, arrived just after ten o'clock, and Henry, happy enough now that he knew the shopping expedition was largely for his benefit, seemed content to stay with her. Eleanor and Margaret had an early lunch and when Fulk got back they were ready and waiting for him.

He had Margaret beside him on their short

journey, apparently enjoying her cheerful chatter, but his manner was remote, although kind enough, when he had occasion to address Eleanor. 'We'll go to my rooms now and from there you can walk to the shops—they're close by and you can't possibly get lost. I shall be ready about four o'clock, so don't bother with tea, we'll have it together before we go home.'

They were in the city now, driving along a street with a wide canal running beside it, but presently Fulk turned into a narrow road which led to a square lined with old red brick houses, before one of which he stopped. 'I'm on the ground floor,' he explained. 'Ring and walk in when you come back.' He got out and opened the doors for them to get out too. 'Go straight across the square and down that passage you can see in that corner, it will bring you out into one of the shopping streets.' He nodded briefly. 'Enjoy your-selves. Forgive me, I'm late,' he told them, and went up the stone steps and in through the front door. As they walked away, Eleanor wondered if he had had any time for lunch; she thought it unlikely.

They had a lovely afternoon, first window-shopping, to gaze at the tempting displays of jewellery, leatherwork, scarves and party clothes suitable for the festive season, but presently, aware that they were quite unable to buy the pink velvet dress Margaret coveted, or the crocodile handbag Eleanor had set her heart upon, they made their modest purchases, handkerchiefs and scarves for the staff at Huys Hensum, a game of Scrabble for Henry as well as a sketchbook and coloured pencils—over Fulk's present they pondered for some time; everything had cost a good deal more than Eleanor had anticipated and many of the things which they might have chosen were far too expensive, but finally they decided on a book. It was *The Ascent of Man* which, Margaret pointed out, he would read with pleasure. 'He's very clever,' she urged, 'and clever people read that kind of book.'

It was while Eleanor was paying for it—and a lot of money it was too—that she noticed her small sister's downcast face. 'What is it, love?' she asked. 'Have you changed your mind—we can easily find something else. . .'

Margaret shook her head. 'No—the book's fine, it's just that I wanted some money to buy something, but we haven't any left, have we?'

Eleanor peered into her purse. She had used up the ten pounds and almost all of the extra money Fulk had advanced her. 'Well, no,' she admitted, 'only a few of those little silver things—*dubbeltjes*, but I tell you what we'll do, we'll go back to Fulk's rooms—it's almost time, anyway, and I'll borrow some more money from him and we can come back quickly and get what you want before we meet him for tea. Will that do?'

They found their way back easily enough to the square, rang the old-fashioned brass bell, and walked in, just as Fulk had told them to do. There was a door on the left of the narrow hall with his name on it and they went in: the waiting room, richly carpeted, nicely furnished, too, with flowers and plenty of magazines—none of your upright chairs and last year's *Woman's Own* laid out like fish on a slab with a gas fire burning economically low. Here the chairs were comfortable, dignified, and upholstered in a pleasing damask in various shades of blue. There were plenty of tables to accommodate handbags, gloves and parcels, too. Eleanor thoroughly approved of it; she approved too of the nice, cosy-looking nurse sitting at her desk; a woman to inspire confidence in the most timid of patients and probably very competent as well. She smiled at them now and spoke in excellent English.

'Professor van Hensum is occupied with

his last patient——if you would seat your-
selves?'

But there was no need, for as she spoke
the door at the other end of the room opened
and a military-looking gentleman marched
out with Fulk just behind him. He went
across to the nurse and said something to her,
exchanged some laughing remark with his
departing patient and went to Eleanor and
Margaret.

'Have you had a good shop?' he wanted
to know. 'I'll be two minutes.' He turned
away, but Margaret slid a hand into his to
stop him. 'Fulk, please will you lend us some
more money? Eleanor hasn't any left and
there's something I want to buy.'

His hand was already in his pocket. 'How
much do you need? Fifty gulden, a hundred?'

'For heaven's sake!' exclaimed Eleanor.
'That's far too much. Margaret, could you
manage with ten gulden, or perhaps fifteen?'

'I tell you what we'll do,' said Fulk easily,
'we'll go along to the shops now and you can
decide how much you want to spend when we
get there. Eleanor, do you want to borrow
any more for yourself?'

She was grateful to him for being so mat-
ter-of-fact about it. There was still some
small thing to choose for Margaret. She did
some hasty mental arithmetic; she had some

more money at Huys Hensum, but not much, and she had no intention of being in his debt. 'Ten gulden would be nice if you could spare it,' she told him, and wondered why he smiled.

She was grateful when they reached the shops, too, for he suggested that she might like to go off on her own while he stayed with Margaret. It left her free to buy the headscarf Margaret had admired before rejoining them outside Vroom and Dreesman's main entrance. Eleanor had to wait a few minutes for them and whiled away the time watching the passers-by thronging the pavements, the women warmly clad with scarves pulled tight against the wind, the children encased in bright woollen outfits, their chubby faces, blue-eyed and pink-cheeked, peering out from under knitted caps, the men, large and solid in thick, short topcoats and a sprinkling of fur caps—and all of them laden with parcels.

Eleanor felt all at once lonely and far from home and her thoughts must have been reflected in her face, for Fulk said at her elbow: 'You're sad, and I wonder why?' He didn't wait for an answer, however, but took them to a nearby café; a cheerful, colourful place, warm and faintly Edwardian with its dark red carpet and panelled walls and little

round tables. They drank their tea and ate
rich cream cakes to the accompaniment of
Margaret's happy chatter, lingering over the
meal so that it was quite dark when they left
the café at length and went back to Fulk's
consulting rooms. During their drive home it
was Margaret who did most of the talking,
and although Fulk laughed and joked with
her readily enough he was absent-minded,
and as for Eleanor, she could think of nothing
to say at all, for her head was full of Fulk.

At the house she went straight to Henry's
room so that the nurse could be freed to return
to Groningen with Fulk. Her brother greeted
her happily, thanked the nurse nicely,
expressed the opinion that he would like to
meet her again, and watched silently while
Eleanor added her own thanks to his together
with a box of chocolates, gaily wrapped.
When the nurse had gone, he asked: 'Why
did you give her a present?'

'Well, it was kind of her to come at such
short notice to keep you company.'

Henry thought this over. 'Yes. She was
nice to Moggy and Flan too. Her name's
Wabke and it's her day off, she told me, but
Fulk asked her to come and sit with me and
she did because she likes him very much,
and he gave her fifty gulden. . .'

'Fifty? Good gracious, I wonder. . .' She

had no chance to worry about whether she should pay him back fifty gulden or not, because Henry asked urgently: 'Did you have tea?'

'Yes, dear.' She had tossed off her hat and coat and gone to sit on the side of his bed.

'So did we. We had a very short walk, just round the house, and then Tekla brought our tea to the sitting room; sandwiches and cake and little biscuits with nuts on them and hot buttered toast. We ate quite a great deal. Wabke says this is a very grand house. Is it, Eleanor?'

'Well, yes, it is rather.' She was still doing sums, wondering if she had enough money to pay Fulk the fifty gulden as well as the money she had borrowed. Henry cut into her calculations with: 'What did you have for tea?'

'Oh, gorgeous cakes,' she brought her mind back with difficulty to their conversation, 'though I think your tea sounded lovely. My cake was chocolate and pineapple and whipped cream arranged on a piece of pastry.'

'What did Margaret have?'

Eleanor was saved from the details by Fulk's entrance. His 'Hullo, old chap, how's the day been?' was uttered in his usual kindly tones, but he didn't look at her at all.

Henry grinned tiredly. 'Super! I like Wabke. Gosh, it's smashing to feel like me again. We went for a walk, you know, ever such a short one, and then we played Ludo and cards, only Wabke isn't very good at games, but she laughs a lot and she liked Moggy and Flan. I hope I shall see her again before I go home.'

'I'll make a note of it,' Fulk assured him gravely, and took his pulse. 'You've done enough for today, though—supper in bed and go to sleep early—remember what I told you? I'll come and see you before I go in the morning.' He glanced at last at Eleanor. 'I shall be out this evening.'

She stopped him at the door. 'Oh—then could you spare a minute. . .?'

'Unless it's urgent, no. I'm late already.' He smiled faintly. 'Good night, Eleanor.'

Which left her feeling snubbed and still fretting about the fifty gulden. And where was he going? It was none of her business, of course, but she did want to know. Being in love, she decided as she got ready for bed some hours later, was no fun at all, and why couldn't she have fallen for someone like Perry Maddon, who liked her for a start, instead of Fulk, who didn't like her at all half the time, and he had far too much money too and led the kind of life she wouldn't enjoy.

That wasn't true; she would enjoy it very much, living in this large, magnificently appointed house, with Juffrouw Witsma and Tekla and Bep to run it. Wearing beautiful clothes too, going out with Fulk to balls and parties, secure in the knowledge that he would come racing home each evening because he couldn't bear to be parted from her. . .the sad feeling inside her which she had managed until now to ignore, dissolved into silent tears.

She didn't go down to breakfast the next morning until she was sure that Fulk had gone, making the excuse to Margaret that Henry had slept late. Her sister gave her a disconcerting stare. 'You've been crying,' she stated. 'You never cry—what's the matter, Eleanor?'

'Nothing, love—I think I'm just a little tired, and I've been so worried about Henry.' Eleanor managed to smile. 'I'll have a cup of coffee and feel fine again. I thought we might write the labels for the presents— Henry could do Fulk's.'

It was a small task, quickly done. She helped Henry, now becoming very independent and inclined to do more than he ought, and then with Margaret, walked in the gardens. There was a nice little wild corner almost out of sight of the house, where there were squirrels and any number of birds. They stopped to feed them and then went on to the pond to feed the ducks. 'What a pity,' Eleanor observed, 'that Fulk has so little time to enjoy his own garden.'

'Oh, but he does,' protested Henry. 'Before I was ill, we used to come here every day after lunch before Fulk went back to his work. Flan came too; we went around looking at things. He must have a lot more patients now, for he doesn't come for lunch any more, does he? He's not often home for tea, either, is he?'

A remark which set Eleanor's unhappy thoughts on an even more unhappy course. It really seemed as though Fulk didn't want to see more of her than he absolutely had to. Perhaps, despite what he had said, Imogen's mother had impressed him with the unwisdom of having her in the house and risking Imogen's feelings being hurt, but in that case, why didn't the girl come back and keep an eye on the situation herself? Not that there was a situation. Eleanor frowned, wondering how much longer it would be before Henry would be fit to travel home; Christmas wasn't far off now and that was a good arguing point. She had already made up her mind to talk to Fulk that evening; she would broach the subject at the same time.

She had no chance until after tea. She had sat on tenterhooks, playing cards with the children while she listened for the car, and when she had at last heard it, she threw in her hand in a manner to bring a flood of remonstrances from her companions, and heedless of their annoyed cries, ran downstairs. She reached the hall as he opened the house door and barely giving him time to get inside, said: 'Fulk, I'd like to speak to you, could it be now?'

He raised his eyebrows. 'If it's as urgent as all that, and presumably it is. You look ready to burst with your feelings, Eleanor. Come into the study.'

He shut the door behind her and waved her to a chair. 'Talk up, dear girl,' he begged her. 'I'll listen, but I've things to do at the same time, if you have no objection.'

It was awkward addressing his broad back while he bent over his desk opening and shutting drawers, taking things out and putting other things away. He looked at the clock too, which hardly encouraged her. Eleanor drew a deep breath. 'It's three things really,' she began ungrammatically. 'I want to know how much money I owe you, and that includes what you paid the nurse who came to look after Henry yesterday, and then I want to know how soon he can go home. . .' She saw him stiffen and hurried on: 'We can never thank you enough for all you've done, but we must be a perfect nuisance to you.' And when he didn't say anything: 'And if he isn't well enough to travel, I'll go if you want me to. I've been thinking, Baroness Oss van Oss was quite right——I mean, about me being here and Imogen not liking it. I wouldn't have liked it either, I'd have come. . .' She paused just in time and changed what she had nearly said to: 'I wouldn't want to——that is, I don't want to upset her even though there's no reason for it, but if I go home you could let her know and she wouldn't mind Henry being here, would she?' She was quite unaware of the pleading in her voice.

She thought she heard Fulk laugh, but of course she must have been mistaken; what was there to laugh about? She sighed a little and waited for him to answer.

He shut a final drawer and leaned against the corner of the desk, jingling his keys gently up and down in one large, well-kept hand.

'You were a tiresome little girl,' he remarked in a gentle voice, 'always wanting to know things, and now that you're grown up you are still tiresome, though perhaps not quite in the same way. I haven't the least idea how much you owe me; when I have the time

I will see about it and let you know, since you will only nag me until I do. And no, Henry is not well enough to go home, and no, I do not wish you to leave my house, and may I add in passing that Baroness Oss van Oss never has and never will influence me in any way. There is only one person who can do that, but she hasn't yet realized that. And now you really must excuse me—I've a date.'

Eleanor stood up too quickly. 'Oh, I didn't know,' she said blankly, and was rendered speechless by his bland: 'How should you? I didn't mention it before.'

She had had no intention of asking, but she heard herself enquiring: 'Are you going away again?'

'Yes. I'll go and see Henry before I leave and if there is anything I think you should know, I'll leave a note on the mantelpiece.'

She said fiercely: 'I don't understand you; you tell me I'm not to go home and yet you make a point of keeping out of my way—I suppose it's for Henry's sake.'

His face was in the shadows. 'Suppose what you like, Eleanor,' he offered calmly, and she turned on her heel and snatched at the door handle.

'I hope you have a nice weekend,' she answered, still fierce, 'although I couldn't care less!' She went through the door and shut it rather violently behind her.

She spent a good deal of the evening trying to cheer up a glum Henry and a disappointed Margaret. 'But he won't be here for Sint Nikolaas,' Henry argued for the tenth time, 'and we've got him a present.'

'He can have it when he gets back,' Eleanor assured him in a cheerful voice which sounded over-loud in her own ears. 'We can give the others their presents and watch the TV, there'll be a special programme and you know you love the colours.'

'But we can't understand what they're saying,' Margaret pointed out in a discouraged voice. 'Do you suppose Fulk forgot?'

'No, of course not, but we have all forgotten that he's engaged to Imogen, and I expect he wants to be with her so that he can give her a present. . .'

'She could have come here,' grumbled Henry. 'I wonder what he'll give her?'

'Rubies and diamonds and emeralds,' stated Margaret positively. 'He's very rich, Hermina told me so. If I were just a little older and he were just a little younger, I should cut Imogen out and marry him myself.' She looked at Eleanor. 'I don't know why you don't, darling Eleanor; you're just a nice age for him and though I've never seen a photograph of her, I'm sure you're a hundred times prettier—besides, wouldn't it be lovely for all of us? We could come and stay with you, and mind the babies while you and Fulk go away on marvellous holidays together. I. . .'

Eleanor knew her voice was sharp. 'Margaret, what nonsense you do talk!' She was helped by Henry's, 'Anyway, you don't like him, do you, Eleanor, you said so in the loft—you said he was a horrid boy.'

'Pooh,' cried Margaret, 'that's a load of hooey, that was years ago; of course you like him, don't you, Eleanor?'

'He's grown into a very kind and—and nice man,' said Eleanor cautiously.

'I wouldn't call him nice, exactly, I mean you don't notice nice people very much, do you? and you do notice Fulk. But he's smashing, all right, his eyes twinkle and he laughs—I mean a real laugh, and when he's cross he goes all quiet instead of shouting.'

Eleanor eyed her sister in some astonishment, agreeing with every word, but all she said was: 'Darling, how observant you are.'

She devised several activities to keep them busy the next morning, and in the afternoon, as it was a fine if cold day, they went for their usual walk before tea, which they had round a splendid fire in the sitting room while they watched the various festivities in honour of the saint. Eleanor switched it off presently, however, because Henry was beginning to look a little tired, and they all went upstairs to his room where she settled him before the fire in a comfortable chair, fetched the games table and suggested that he and Margaret might like to have a game of draughts while she went to the kitchen to see what was for his supper. She had turned the angle of the staircase and had paused to admire the prospect of the hall below her when the front door opened and her mother and father walked in, followed by Fulk.

Her joyous cry of 'Fulk!' she drowned very quickly by her breathless exclamation of: 'Mother, Father!' as she raced down the staircase to fling herself at her smiling parents. 'Oh, what a glorious surprise!' she babbled. 'Won't Henry and Margaret be thrilled—they're up in his room.' She looked at Fulk then. 'I thought you'd gone to spend Sint Nikolaas with Imogen.'

He said nothing, although he smiled and his dark eyes held a gleam which might have been anger, or possibly amusement as he suggested to Mrs MacFarlane that they might like to see Henry before they did anything else.

After that the evening went like a bomb.

Henry, so excited that he could hardly speak, consented to lie down on his bed and rest on the understanding that he should join the rest of the party for dinner later on, and Margaret undertook to unpack for her mother, never ceasing to talk as she did so. Fulk had taken Mr MacFarlane down to the sitting room for a drink, suggesting that the ladies might like a cup of tea upstairs, 'For you'll want to gossip,' he declared, 'and there's plenty of time before dinner.'

Eleanor was left to coax Henry to rest, to tidy away the children's game and then to follow her mother and sister to the big bedroom in the front of the house, where she sat on the bed, joining in the conversation and pouring the tea when it came. It wasn't until the evening was over, with Henry safely tucked up in bed and the rest of them saying their good nights, that she had a moment alone with Fulk. The other three had gone across the hall to look at a particular portrait in the dining-room which they had been talking about, leaving Fulk lounging by the french window in the drawing room, waiting for Flan to come in, and Eleanor, standing, very erect, by the door. She plunged into speech at once, for there was no knowing how long they might be left alone, and although she had thought over what she was going to say, she realized now that she had forgotten every word; better get it over with. She relaxed a little and said soberly:

'Fulk, I must thank you for all the trouble you've taken to bring Mother and Father here, and the expense and the time—I only wish you were as happy as we all feel.'

He had turned his head to watch her. Now he said blandly: 'It merely required a telephone call or two, a couple of free days which I had owing to me, anyway, and as to the expense, I'm sure that by now someone must have told you that I am a wealthy man.'

'Well—yes, Hermina told Margaret and she told me, but you could have had all the money in the world and still not done it.' She gulped, 'Oh, I feel so mean—you see, I thought you'd gone to Cannes again, to your Imogen, and I was beastly enough to mind about it, and that's where you should be really, not here with us. You could have gone out dancing and dining and having fun.' She went on feverishly, seeing it all in her mind's eye. 'There would be sunshine, wouldn't there, and you could have gone riding too and given each other presents, and. . .'

His short laugh stopped her, his voice was all silk. 'Hardly that. Imogen considers the feast of Sint Nikolaas old-fashioned.' He smiled with a trace of mockery while she tried to find something to say and then went on, still silkily: 'When we came in this evening, you cried my name—oh, you remembered to cover it up quickly, but not quite quickly enough. Why, Eleanor?'

She had hoped that he hadn't heard. She said lamely: 'I was surprised; I thought you were miles away. . .'

He came and stood in front of her, but she didn't look at him. 'It's nice to think that I'm on your mind, even when I'm not here.' He laughed again, quite cheerfully this time. 'Although perhaps it was those few guldens you owe me which were on your mind—was that it?'

She seized on that, thankful for an excuse, and then, anxious to get away from him, embarked on a disjointed speech which became more and more muddled as she went along, happily unaware of the unholy delight in his eyes. She was brought to a sudden stop by his kiss. 'Your thoughts show very plainly on your pretty face, my dear,' he told her gently, and opened the door and ushered her out.

CHAPTER NINE

SINT NIKOLAAS would be coming in the evening after tea, which meant that the day was spent, by Henry and Margaret at least, in a state of anticipation. With the exception of Eleanor and her brother, the whole party went to church in the morning, and for the benefit of Mr MacFarlane, Fulk drove them to Groningen to the Martinikerk, so that during lunch the conversation largely concerned this magnificent edifice with its sixteenth-century wall paintings in the choir and its five-storied spire. 'A pity that you were unable to see it for yourself, my dear,' remarked Eleanor's father. 'Should you go to Groningen before you return to Scotland, you must make a point of visiting it.' He turned to Fulk. 'I was much struck by the architecture of the village church we passed on our way home—in the Roman-Gothic style, I fancy.'

Eleanor, eating her delicious ragout of game, wondered if Fulk was bored; he didn't appear to be, indeed, he seemed to know as much about the building of churches as her father did. She listened to him telling her father that that particular style of building was only to be found in the most northerly provinces of the country, and entering into a discussion concerning the differences between the early and late Gothic style of architecture, but he was too well-mannered to allow their talk to monopolize the conversation and switched easily enough to other matters, and soon everyone was talking in a more lighthearted fashion, especially Henry, who, having been a very good boy all the morning, was now inclined to get excited; something which Eleanor saw quickly enough; so did Fulk, for as soon as lunch was finished and before they all went into the drawing room for their coffee, he suggested in the mildest of voices that Henry should have his afternoon rest a little earlier than usual. 'You don't want to miss Sint Nikolaas' arrival,' he pointed out, 'and if you take a nap now, you will be downstairs again in plenty of time for tea.'

Henry agreed cheerfully enough and Eleanor bore her small brother away, tucked him up, admonished him in sisterly tones to be good, and went back to the drawing room, where she spent the rest of the afternoon listening to her mother's quiet voice talking about the various small happenings at home, and answering suitably when she was expected to. But she left most of the talking to Margaret, who had a great deal to say and had them all laughing over her various experiences, for unlike Eleanor, she had been to the village on various occasions, had tea at Hermina's home, and spent a good deal of time with Juffrouw Witsma in the kitchen, watching her cook and learning Dutch at the same time. It was Fulk who remarked: 'I'm afraid that Eleanor hasn't had the same opportunities as Margaret, for she has been tied hand and foot to Henry. I don't know what I should have done without her help, for I have been able to go about my daily work knowing that he was safe with her.'

They all looked at her, and she looked at her shoes, feeling foolish, and her mother said thoughtfully: 'Well, we shall have to make it up to her in some way,' and smiled across at Fulk as she spoke, and he agreed with a smile before enquiring about Mrs Trot. 'Moggy fits very well into our household,' he observed, 'and Flan adores him.' The big dog lifted his head and thumped his tail, drawing attention to himself, and the talk, naturally enough, turned to dogs.

Tea was over and everyone was sitting round talking in a desultory fashion when there was a thunderous knock on the door, and Henry, who had been sitting silently with his ears cocked for the slightest sound, got out of his chair. Fulk got up too, observing that Sint Nikolaas was punctual as usual and they had better see what he had left at the door, and with Henry beside him, went out of the room, to return very shortly with a large, bulging sack. He set it down in the centre of the room, saying: 'Margaret, go to the kitchen and fetch everyone here, will you? and then you and Henry shall hand round the presents.'

There were gifts for everyone there, even for Mr and Mrs MacFarlane, a thoughtful act on Fulk's part which engendered Eleanor's instant gratitude, and when the sack was at last empty, Henry, being the youngest person present, was allowed to open his parcels first.

He opened each gift carefully, and there were quite a number, for besides the presents Eleanor and Margaret had bought, there were a variety of things to please a small boy, and the last package of all, an air gun, complete with pellets and a target board, caused him to shout with delight.

'We'll fix the target up tomorrow,' Fulk promised, and Henry, for all his clever little brain still uncertain about the good saint who handed out presents so lavishly, asked: 'How could Sint Nikolaas possibly know that I wanted a gun?'

Fulk shrugged his broad shoulders. 'It's something most boys want. When you've got the hang of it we'll do some clay pigeon shooting, if you like. Now it's Margaret's turn.'

The pink velvet dress she had so much admired was at the bottom of the pile. She shook it free from its folds of tissue paper and all she could say was: 'Oh, Fulk—it's the dress I showed you when we were shopping in Groningen!' She ran across the room and flung her arms round his neck and kissed him soundly. 'Oh, you really are groovy,' she told him fervently, and raced away to try it on.

By the time it came to Eleanor's turn, everyone was in high spirits; somehow Fulk had managed to create the right atmosphere of excitement and pleasure and the traditional wine they were drinking certainly helped him. She began on the little pile before her, feeling like a child again; the crocodile handbag was in the third box she opened; the very one she had admired with Margaret, and her sister, a charming picture in her new pink dress and perched on the side of Fulk's chair, called out: 'I pointed it out to Fulk, Eleanor, but I never knew—honestly I didn't.'

It was a beautiful thing; Eleanor had never had anything like it before, probably she never would again. She laid it down carefully and looked at Fulk, watching her. 'Thank you,' she said in a voice which quavered a little, 'it's marvellous—you shouldn't have done it, but it's quite—quite. . .' Words failed her when he asked, laughing:

'Don't I get the same treatment as Margaret gave me?'

There was a little wave of laughter and there was really no way out. She crossed the room and kissed him, aware of the eyes watching her. The kiss was light and brief and she managed some sort of laughing remark before she sat down again and opened the rest of the presents she had been given; it was a relief when she got to the last one and everyone turned their attention to Juffrouw Witsma, whose turn it was.

Being the master of the house, Fulk opened his gifts last of all. His devoted staff had given him handkerchiefs and a rather dreadful tie which he declared was exactly to his taste; Eleanor had no doubt that he would wear it just because they had given it to him, although the blinding paisley pattern was hardly his style. He opened the book last of all, declaring that it was just what he had intended getting for himself, and then went round thanking everyone; when he reached Eleanor his thanks were brief. 'I've kissed all the other women,' he told her in a soft voice, 'but I'm not going to kiss you, Eleanor—and you're welcome to make what you like of that.'

He grinned suddenly at her before going to open the champagne without which he declared Sint Nikolaas Avond was incomplete.

Everything was back to normal in the morning; Eleanor got down to breakfast to find Fulk already behind his paper, and although he wished her good morning, his detached manner gave her the impression that for him at least life was real, life was earnest. There was no one else there and he seemed to feel no need for conversation, but continued to read *De Haagsche Post* while he finished his coffee. Presently he folded it carefully, gathered up his letters, said good-bye to her in the tones of a man who was simply upholding the conventions, mentioned that he would see Henry before he left for the hospital, and went from the room, leaving her feeling strangely hollow. Not that she allowed her feelings to overcome her; when her family joined her a few minutes later, she was the life and soul of the breakfast table.

Mr and Mrs MacFarlane were to stay a week, and it had already been decided that Henry should remain where he was until a few days before Christmas. He was doing well now, but as Fulk had pointed out, he was living in a strict routine now, with long rest periods, early bedtime and a kind but firm refusal to indulge any ambitious whims he might think up. The longer he kept to this routine, the better chance he had of permanent recovery, and when his parents protested that the boy was giving Fulk a great deal of trouble he shrugged it off with: 'Not in the least. I have already told you that Eleanor takes the brunt of caring for him, and heaven knows the house is large enough for us all.'

A remark, which, when relayed to Eleanor, did nothing to improve her spirits. She and her mother were walking in the garden and Mrs MacFarlane, having delivered this facer, went on: 'Such a good, kind man; he will make a splendid husband. I wonder what this Imogen of his is like? I would have thought that she would have wanted to spend more time with him. . .'

'Fulk went to see her,' Eleanor explained in a calm little voice, 'just for the weekend— he must love her very much to go all that way just for a weekend. . .'

'There are other reasons for taking long

journeys,' remarked her parent, and before Eleanor could ask her what she meant, she asked: 'What about you, darling? Will you have to go straight back to the hospital, or will you be able to come home for Christmas?'

'I hadn't thought about it.' And it was true, she hadn't. 'I'd better write and find out, hadn't I? Though I'm sure they'll expect me, you know what Christmas is like on the wards, and I wouldn't dare be away.' She fell silent, contemplating Christmas without Fulk, and not only Christmas; the rest of the year, and all the years after that.

It was during dinner that evening that Fulk remarked to the table in general that he thought that Eleanor deserved a day out. 'And now that you are here,' he suggested pleasantly, 'she could quite safely have one, could she not?' He addressed Mr MacFarlane. 'She would have the chance to see the Martinikerk for herself, and there are one or two splendid museums. I have arranged to take a day so that I may go with her.'

He smiled round the table and everyone, with the exception of Eleanor, smiled back, agreeing with him in a pleased chorus, not realizing that the subject of this treat hadn't been given a chance to accept or refuse it.

During the animated discussion which followed as to the best way of cramming as much as possible into a day's outing, Eleanor remained silent; not that anyone noticed; they were all too busy putting forward their own views as to what constituted the highlights of sightseeing. Her father, naturally enough, had a good deal to say about churches, and the Martinikerk in particular, but he was drowned by Margaret's insistent voice raised on behalf of old castles, and her mother, a poor third, voiced the view that perhaps a nice look at the shops would be the thing. Fulk, sitting back in his chair, listened courteously to their arguments, saying little, while he watched Eleanor, but presently he gathered the threads of the conversation skilfully together in such a way that each felt that he or she had contributed a valuable piece of advice and suggested that they should go into the drawing room for coffee. It was a chance that Eleanor took. Mumbling that she would see if Henry was comfortable, she flew upstairs, where she spent quite an unnecessary amount of time shaking up her brother's pillows while she tried to decide what to do. A day out with Fulk would be heaven, there could be no argument about that; on the other hand, he hadn't asked her, had he? Not in so many words. He was making a gesture, rewarding her for her long hours in the sick-room. Well, she didn't want a reward! She gave the surprised Henry's pillow still another shake and went downstairs. The drawing room door was shut and she could hear voices and laughter from behind it; she suddenly didn't want to go in and half turned on the staircase to go to her room when Fulk's study door opened and he put his head out.

'Ah, I thought so—I could practically smell the paintwork blistering under your bad temper.'

'I am not in a bad temper!'

'Come in, then—we'll have a cosy chat.'

She stayed exactly where she was. 'What about?'

'Our day out tomorrow, of course.'

She looked down her nose at him. 'I wasn't aware that I had been invited to go anywhere with anyone,' she informed him coldly.

'Quite right, dear Eleanor, you haven't. You would have refused point blank, wouldn't you, but now that everyone has gone to such trouble to suggest where we should go, and your mother is here to look after Henry, you can't very well refuse, can you?'

'I can't think why you should want to spend a day with me.'

His eyes narrowed. 'Coming from any other girl, I wouldn't believe a word of that,' he told her blandly, 'but from you. . .' His voice became friendly and warm. 'I haven't had a day out myself for a long time. I need a break.'

She said instantly: 'You went to Cannes to see Imogen.'

He agreed affably, and then: 'You're a little old-fashioned, Eleanor.'

'I'm very old-fashioned, if you want to know. We don't move very fast with the times where I come from.'

'So I realized. It may astonish you to know that the people around these parts don't either—very behind the times, we are. Now, having settled that to our mutual satisfaction, will you spend the day with me tomorrow, Eleanor?'

She knew then that she had never intended doing anything else but that; let the absent Imogen look after herself; she had no one else to blame and she must be a very conceited girl if she didn't imagine that Fulk might need a little female society from time to time. She said frankly:

'I'd like to very much, thank you, Fulk.'

It was pouring with rain when she got up the next morning; cold heavy rain rattling down like a steel curtain from a uniformly grey sky. Eleanor stood looking at it from her bedroom window, resigned to the fact that there would be no day out. It didn't look any better from Henry's room either; she was finishing off a few small chores for him when Fulk walked in. His good morning was cheerful. 'I hope you like rain,' he observed cheerfully, 'for we're going to get plenty of it today—the wind's cold too, so wear a thick coat, you can keep dry under my umbrella.'

She found herself smiling. 'I didn't think we'd be going. . .'

He looked surprised. 'Why not? You don't strike me as being one of those girls who fuss at getting a bit wet.'

She assured him happily that indeed she wasn't fussy, and went down to breakfast in the best of spirits.

Looking back at the end of the day, she wasn't sure which part of it she had enjoyed most; the great church had been wonderful— all that space and loftiness, so had the Municipal Museum, where she had spent a long time gazing at the regional costumes. They had had coffee afterwards in the Grand Hotel Frigge and then gone on to look at the university, which she found too modern for her taste, although the variety of coloured caps worn by the students intrigued her.

They had left Fulk's car outside his rooms

and walked through the rain, arm-in-arm under Fulk's umbrella, for that was the only way in which to see the city properly, he told her. They went through the narrow streets between the two main squares, pausing to admire the variety of old houses lining the canals, peering down centuries-old alleys, looking down into the cold grey water from the small bridges as they crossed them. It was on one of these that Fulk had quite suddenly kissed her, one arm sweeping her close, the other still holding the umbrella and even in this rather awkward situation, he contrived to carry out the exercise with an expertise which took her breath. She had looked up at him, rain dripping down her pretty face, a little flushed now, uneasily aware that she had kissed him back, if not expertly, at least with enthusiasm.

'You're very pretty in the rain,' Fulk had said, and taken her by the arm and walked her on through the almost empty little streets, pointing out anything of interest with an ease of manner which made her wonder if he made a habit of kissing girls on bridges whenever he felt like it. She wondered if she should make some lighthearted remark to that effect, but she had been unable to think of one; silence was probably the best thing, with of course, suitable observations about the house he was telling her about.

They went back to the car after a little while and drove up to the coast to Warffrum, where there was a castle converted into a hotel. They had lunched there, beginning with *Erwten* soup to warm them up and going on to sole Murat and Charlotte Russe, sitting over their coffee until the afternoon sky began to darken from grey to black and Fulk suggested that for the last hour or two she might like to look round the shops in Groningen, something she was very willing to do, although she had been very careful not to express admiration for any article which caught her fancy; she wasn't sure, but if he could buy a crocodile handbag just because she had admired it, he could just as likely purchase any of the trifles which caught her eye, so she confined her admiration to the fabulously expensive jewellery, taking care to remark a cool 'How nice,' to anything she judged to be within his pocket.

She was quite unaware that her painstaking efforts were affording her companion a good deal of amusement, but she found it a relief when he suggested that they might have tea before they went back home, and she agreed readily enough when he had asked her if it would be a good idea to buy Henry a book about air pistols and guns. At the same time he had bought a box of chocolates for Margaret, pointing out gravely that children should be treated equally, an opinion which she shared and which occupied them pleasantly as they drove back.

They had rounded off the day with a hilarious game of Monopoly after dinner, and Henry, for a treat, had been allowed to stay up until nine o'clock. The rest of them had stayed up much longer than that and the great Friese wall clock in the hall was chiming midnight when they went to their beds. Eleanor, lingering to thank Fulk for her day, had been a little chilled by the cool courtesy of his reply, so that she had gone up to bed wondering if his apparent enjoyment of it had been nothing but good manners. But surely mere good manners didn't necessitate kissing her in the middle of a bridge?

The week went very quickly after that; it was Friday evening again in no time at all, with her parents packed and ready to leave and Fulk, whom she had hardly seen during the last few days, wishing her goodbye with the unwelcome information that he wouldn't be coming straight back this time. 'There's a seminar in Edinburgh on Monday,' he told her, 'and I hope to attend it; I shan't be back until the middle of the week. You know what to do for Henry and if you are in the least worried you can telephone me. Have you any messages?'

She couldn't think of one. She kissed her parents goodbye and wished them all a safe journey, wanting with all her heart to be free to go with them. The house was very quiet when they had gone; the children went to bed and she was left to roam round on her own, a prey to her thoughts, picturing Fulk at her home, driving down to Edinburgh, meeting people she didn't know, living a life in which she had no share. She went to bed at last, feeling lost.

He came back on Wednesday evening and almost as soon as he had entered his front door the telephone rang, and Eleanor, who had heard the car arriving and had come into the hall, paused.

'Yes, answer it, there's a good girl,' he begged her, 'while I get out of this coat.'

She went into the study and lifted the receiver gingerly, hoping that whoever was the other end wouldn't break into a torrent of Dutch. She said: 'Hullo?' which could do no harm anyway and a girl's voice answered, a sharp voice asking a sharp question.

'Wait a minute,' said Eleanor in English. 'Professor van Hensum is just back, I'll call him.'

The voice spoke English now. 'You are Eleanōr? You are still there. . .' There was a tinkling laugh. 'Fetch Fulk, tell him it is Imogen.'

He was strolling across the hall to take the receiver from her. 'Who is it?' he asked, 'or is it someone speaking double dutch?'

'It's Imogen.' She didn't wait, but went out of the room, closing the door carefully behind her and going back to Henry and Margaret. She had often imagined Imogen's voice, and now she had heard it; it merely served to confirm her opinion of the girl. She embarked on a game of spillikins with the children and when presently Fulk joined them, Imogen wasn't mentioned.

She met him at breakfast the next morning; Henry still had his breakfast in bed and Margaret had taken Flan for a walk and beyond an exchange of good mornings they had nothing to say to each other, only as Fulk went from the room he told her: 'I have no idea when I shall be home, if you want me urgently, telephone the hospital.' His smile was brief, although she heard him whistling cheerfully as he went out of the house.

It was almost tea time when Eleanor, leaving Margaret to entertain Henry, went down to the kitchen to fetch the tea tray; if Fulk wasn't coming home there seemed no point in making a lot of extra work. She was crossing the hall when the front door bell rang and she went to see who it was. Juffrouw Witsma was in her room and Tekla would be busy in the kitchen. A girl stood outside and before Eleanor could utter a word had pushed past her into the hall. A quite beautiful girl, wrapped in a fur coat, her guinea-gold hair tucked up under a little fur cap, her legs encased in the kind of boots Eleanor had always wanted and never been able to afford. She walked into the centre of the hall before she said in English: 'Where is Fulk?'

'You're Imogen,' declared Eleanor, not answering. She got a cold look for her pains.

'Naturally.' She frowned. 'This filthy weather, how I hate it, and this frightful barn of a house. . .'

'It's a very beautiful house,' said Eleanor sharply, 'and it can't be summer all the year round.'

'Oh, yes, it can.' Imogen walked back to where Eleanor was standing and stared at her, rather as though she were a piece of furniture or something at a fair. 'I came to see you. Mama said that you were pretty, and I suppose you are in a large way, but not in the least chic—I wonder what Fulk sees in you?'

'Nothing,' said Eleanor quickly, 'nothing

at all—he's in love with you.'

Imogen smiled, her lovely mouth curling in a sneer. 'Rubbish! You are—how do you say?—dim. Well, I have seen you for myself; I shall go.' She walked to the door and actually had her hand on its handle when Eleanor cried: 'But you can't—Fulk won't be long, at least I don't think so; he usually comes home after tea. Couldn't you telephone his rooms or the hospital and tell him you're here?'

Imogen was pulling her coat collar close. 'Why should I wish to see him?'

'But you're going to marry him—you love him,' declared Eleanor, persevering.

'No, I'm not, and I don't.' Imogen disappeared in a whirl of fur, only her expensive perfume lingering after her as she crashed the heavy door shut.

'Well,' said Eleanor on a long-drawn breath, 'now what?'

It was at that precise moment that she turned her head and saw Fulk standing in the doorway of his study, his shoulders wedged comfortably against the door jamb, his hands in his pockets.

'There you are!' she exclaimed. 'Just in time—for heaven's sake go after her. It's Imogen—if you run. . .'

'My dear Eleanor,' said Fulk calmly, 'I

never run, and even if I went after her, what would I say?'

'Why, that you love her, of course.'

'But I don't.'

Her brows drew together in a quite fierce frown. 'But you're going to marry her.'

He smiled a little. 'I heard Imogen tell you in no uncertain terms that she wasn't going to marry me.'

She gave him a scornful look. 'Women always say things like that. I expect she's walking down the road crying her eyes out.'

'Not Imogen; she'll have a taxi waiting.'

'Don't quibble—what does it matter, taxi or walking. . .'

'It doesn't matter at all,' he agreed placidly. 'I can't think why you're making such a business of the whole thing.'

She was bewildered, but she wasn't going to give up. Later on, when she was alone again, she could nurse her broken heart. 'But you're. . .!' she began again.

'If you are going to tell me once more—erroneously—that I love Imogen, I shall do you a mischief.' His voice was still unworried. 'I haven't been in love with her for quite some time—since, in fact, I climbed the ladder to the loft and saw you sitting there in your old clothes and your hair streaming. . . You looked—well, never mind that for the moment. And Imogen—she has never loved me, you know, I imagine that she was flattered at the idea of being mistress of this house and having all the money she wanted, but love—no, my dear. All the same, I had to be certain, didn't I? That's why I went to see her; I don't think I was surprised and certainly not in the least upset to find that she was—er—consoling herself with an American millionaire—short and fat and going bald, but still a millionaire.' He added almost apologetically: 'An American millionaire is so much richer than a Dutch one, you know.'

'You're not a millionaire?' Eleanor wanted to know.

'Well, yes—at least, in Holland, I am.' He strolled across the hall towards her. 'I suppose if I were to offer you this house and my millions you would kick them right back at me, Eleanor?'

'Yes.' She had seen the look on his face, and although her heart begged her to stay just where she was, she took a prudent step backwards.

But he had seen that. 'No, don't move, my darling; it would not be of the least use, you know, I should only come after you.' He smiled at her and her unhappy heart became whole once more.

'If I offered you my heart and my love would you throw them back at me too?' he asked.

'No.' Her voice was a whisper. There was no mistaking the look upon his face now. She took another step back and felt the stairs against her heel. She had reached the second tread when she was halted by his: 'Come down off the staircase, dear Eleanor.'

She supposed she would always do what he wanted her to do from now on. She reached the floor once more and he took her hands in his.

'Oh, my dear darling,' he said, 'come into the little sitting room,' and he opened the door and drew her gently inside. The whole charming place smelled delicious; there was an enormous bunch of red roses lying on the table and Eleanor cried: 'Oh, how glorious!' and wrinkled her charming nose in delight.

'Roses for Christmas,' said Fulk, 'just to prove that you do mean something to someone, my dear love.' He pulled a tatty piece of paper from his pocket. 'The last thing on your list, though I promise you they will be the first of many.'

He pulled her close. 'It's been you all the time, my darling. How strange it is that one can love someone and not know it.' He bent to kiss her, not once, but several times and slowly. 'Of course, boys of sixteen don't always know these things.'

She looked at him enquiringly and he kissed her again. 'You were almost five, sweetheart; I pulled your hair and you kicked my shins and fell over, do you remember? And when I picked you up you were warm and grubby and soft and you cried all over me; I lost my heart then, but never knew it.'

His arm tightened around her. 'Will you marry me, Eleanor? And you had better say yes, for I shan't let you go until you do.'

Eleanor heaved a sigh. 'Oh, Fulk, of course I will—and don't ever let me go.' She leaned up to kiss him and sighed again; she had never been so happy. 'I wonder. . .' she began dreamily, and was interrupted by the opening of the door.

'Juffrouw Witsma has made a cake,' Henry informed them, 'and I'm rather hungry. Do you suppose I might have a slice?'

Fulk still had tight hold of Eleanor. 'Certainly you may—two slices if you wish, and give Margaret some too—and don't hurry too much over eating it.'

'Thank you.' Henry looked at them with interest. 'Are you kissing Eleanor, Fulk?'

'Indeed I am.'

'Are you going to marry her?'

'We were discussing that when you came in.'

'I can take a hint,' said Henry in a tolerant voice. 'I suppose you won't mind if I just mention it to Margaret?'

'By all means do so.' Fulk's voice gave no sign of impatience, but perhaps Henry saw something in his eye, for he turned to go. 'There's a bowl of fruit on the sideboard,' he informed them. 'Might we have an apple too? If we have to wait while you talk, we may get hungry.'

'Eat any of the fruit you fancy,' Fulk told him, and when the door had shut: 'Now, where had I got to? I think perhaps, if you agree, my darling, I'll begin again from the beginning; I rather enjoyed hearing you say that you would marry me.'

Eleanor lifted her head from his shoulder. There was really no need to say anything to that. She smiled and kissed him instead.

MILLS & BOON®

Back by Popular Demand

BETTY NEELS

COLLECTOR'S EDITION

A collector's edition of favourite titles from one of the world's best-loved romance authors.

Mills & Boon are proud to bring back these sought after titles, now reissued in beautifully matching volumes and presented as one cherished collection.

Don't miss these unforgettable titles, coming next month:

Title #17 THE LITTLE DRAGON
Title #18 THE SILVER THAW

Available wherever
Mills & Boon books are sold

MILLS & BOON®

BETTY NEELS

COLLECTOR'S EDITION

If you have missed any of the previously published titles in the Betty Neels Collector's Edition, you may order them by sending a cheque or postal order (please do not send cash) made payable to Harlequin Mills & Boon Ltd. for £2.99 per book plus 50p postage and packing for the first book and 25p for each additional book. Please send your order to: Betty Neels Collector's Edition, P.O. Box 236, Croydon, Surrey, CR9 3RU (EIRE: Betty Neels Collector's Edition, P. O. Box 4546, Dublin 24).

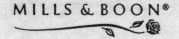